On Harbor's Edge

BOOK ONE: 1912–1913

KATE HOTCHKISS

On Harbor's Edge
Book One: 1912–1913
Copyright © 2020 Kate Hotchkiss

ISBN: 978-1-63381-227-7

This is a work of fiction. Names, characters, places, and incidents either are the product of the author's imagination or are used fictitiously, and any resemblance to actual persons, living or dead, is coincidental.

Cover art and illustrations by:
Scott Hewett Fine Art

Cover design, book design, and production by:
Maine Authors Publishing
12 High Street, Thomaston, Maine
www.maineauthorspublishing.com

Printed in the United States of America

For the loves of my life, in order of arrival
Ethan, Caleb, Ellard

Gratitude

Susan Conley

I am eternally grateful to award-winning, critically-acclaimed author and friend Susan Conley. Susan's brilliant, patient editing of *On Harbor's Edge* made the story soar. I am honored by her interest and a better writer for her instruction.

Books by Conley:

Elsey Come Home
Foremost Good Fortune
Landslide (Knopf, February 2021)
Maine: Life in a Day (Introduction)
Paris Was the Place
Stop Here, This Is the Place

Acknowledgments

Linda Greenlaw
Award-winning author, fisherman, and mother
Thank you, Linda, for the kick!

Scott Hewett
I am astounded by Scott Hewett's illustrations and talent.
Thank you, Scott, for the magic!

Spannocchia Group
Sarah Claytor, Chrissy Conley, Susan Conley, Ellen Davis,
Amy Dempsey, Anna Dibble, James Hook, Julie Kingsley,
Lily King, Benjamin Rubenstein, Carter Walker
Thank you, writers, for the inspiration!

Abbe Museum, Julia Allison, Jean Archibald, Abdelqader Bakir, Hytham Bakir, Patricia Bakir, Billy Barter, Anne & Louis Blaisdell, Lydia Brown, Stephanie Cabot, Kendra Chubbuck, Bernard Cornwell, Lily Crane, Genie Dailey, Jenn Dean, Jessica Dückert, Andy Gelinas, Nikki Giglia, Ernest Hemingway, Diane Hewett, Wendy Higgins, Audrey Hotchkiss, Jeffrey Hotchkiss, Melissa Hotchkiss, Sarah Hotchkiss, Annie Hwang, Isle au Haut Historical Society, Dan Karker, Jane Karker, Starr Kelly, Nan Lee, Maine Authors Publishing, Maine Writers & Publishers Alliance, Caleb Mao, Ethan Mao, Areen Nakhleh, Jean Newberry, North Haven Historical Society, North Haven Library, Eileen O'Conner, Kate Quinn, Elizabeth Rossano, Vincent Rossano, Elisabeth Schmitz, Lisa Shields, David Taylor, Ellard Taylor, Avery Waterman, Elliot Williams, Judy Wood, Anna Worrall
Thank you, all, for the contributions!

"Got to hurry this!" Thaddeus Gale yelled. The warm June wind blew dark hair over his blue eyes. He steadied the boat with one hand, the other waving me forward, the cold Atlantic sloshing about his leather boots.

I did not get into the boat.

"Don't seem too bad out there," ventured my father. "My dear fellow, stay a while. You're family now, for Christ's sake."

"Not here. Other end. Popplestone's going to get hit something fierce. There's a gale coming! Can't you smell it?"

No, dear me no, I did not want to get into the boat.

"Then stay here the night, my man. A new son-in-law is most welcome. You're just rowing, by God!"

"Mildred May needs to see her house."

"Yes, but—" my father nearly wailed.

I watched Pa kick a couple of stones, quiet. He stood on the very same spot where Thaddeus had proposed for the fifth time seven months earlier, late November of 1911. My family and friends lined the sandy beach, the field beyond them windswept into waves.

"Mildred May Combs Gale!" yelled Thaddeus. "Storm's not going to wait for us!"

I eyed the vessel.

Mother interrupted my silence. "Mildred May, I know what you're thinking. You'll be fine. He's got himself a peapod. Seas won't pour over her stern, like what happened with Otto's pa's boat."

"Mildred May!" Thaddeus bellowed.

"But I have never been away from my island!" I shrieked.

"One more time, I'd like to offer my home," Pa tried.

"Thank you kindly," Thaddeus said, curt yet softer. "Got to go. Now. Sorry about the reception. You all enjoy it for us."

"We will." Pa was defeated.

"I do not even have time to change!" The outer layer of my wedding dress flapped in the breeze, thwacking like fresh sheets on a washing line. Even the short jacket covering my high-necked lace bodice blew about some, despite ribbons tying it together for modesty. My fancy swept-up hair fell apart in the breeze, Ma's carefully placed clips hanging by their ends.

"You look a vision in that dress," chirped Ma. "Should wear it as long as you can. Turn some captains' heads if you meet up with anyone crossing Silver Bay. Some cunnin' you are."

I grabbed Ma's elbow and pulled her away from Thaddeus and the rest of the family, my ivory gown dragging over seaweed-covered rocks, staining its delicate edges a light orange. When we reached a small spruce on the upper edge of the shore, I whined, "I do not know what to do!"

My ma, stunning in her bright-yellow dress tied at the waist with a thick pink bow, lit up with a grin. "Don't you worry none, Mr. Gale will teach you everything you need to know. Comes naturally, you'll see."

"What if I do not see?"

"Trust me, you will."

Trust me for my ma meant end of conversation.

I lifted the dress above my rubber boots and entered the water. I had never been in a boat. Never been off my island.

My new husband took off his wedding coat and tie, still dashing in a crisp white shirt and black slacks. He rolled up his sleeves, revealing sun-darkened muscles honed from hauling lobster traps since he was a boy. *Good heavens...perhaps Ma was right...*

I got into the stern. Which promptly settled on the bottom. The bow bobbed like a tethered horse trying to get free.

"Too heavy, get out!" Thaddeus ordered.

I climbed out, not bothering to hold up my dress.

Thaddeus and my two uncles pushed the peapod deeper as I followed, one hand on the gunwale. Pa dashed into the water and held me steady.

In thigh-deep seas with my dress billowing about, I could not get into the boat. My feet stung in that icy water as if stabbed with a knife, and the dress was hung up on something. My father, shorter than me, was of no use. I looked about, not sure what to do, but Thaddeus pushed Pa aside, grabbed the dress, and with a firm yank, freed it from the keel. He then thrust one arm into the ocean under my knees, placed the other at my back, and lifted swiftly. The man dropped me into the boat, not in gentle fashion. The vessel shook, and then she floated. I held the jagged tear in the train of my dress for a moment, and then took off my boots to pour out that cold ocean.

"Got to hurry this!" he commanded again.

My uncles tied the dory's painter to the peapod's stern. Pa had given us that scrapper of a boat when he saw that my belongings would not all easily fit in Thaddeus's.

A gaggle of friends and family waved so madly, seemed their arms might fly right off their shoulders.

"Got to go, Mrs. Gale. Finish your goodbyes."

I waved. Pa wiped a tear as he backed into shallower water, not taking his eyes off me. Ma positively glowed.

I could not find my sister Julia.

We set out, sun high overhead, hampered by the dory weighted with trunks. A few more distant "Byes!" and "Good lucks!" and the crowd headed off to enjoy my wedding cake and to talk about us.

My youngest brother lagged behind. Four-year-old Foster waved, his other hand in his pocket. I smiled, waved back, and blew him a kiss. The kiss "hit" his freckly face, and he stepped back with its imagined strength. I laughed, took a deep breath, blew him a pile more with two hands, and watched him fall over when they struck.

Foster stood up with a grin, followed by tears he wiped away with his forearm. Julia ran out of the woods then, kneeled, and hugged him.

She rose, took his hand, then both turned and chased after the others, Julia looking back for the briefest of moments.

And it was my turn to cry.

"Thaddeus?"

"Yes?"

"Please tell me where we are."

"You know how far Crescent is from the mainland, don't you?"

"About three miles."

"Popplestone's another eleven nautical miles out."

"My word! Over twelve miles! And the closest town?"

"You mean in America?"

"America?"

"America is what Popplestoners call the mainland."

"I see. Yes, in America."

"Graniteville ain't quite in America, is on Robin Isle, a big island right close to the mainland."

"Is there a bridge between Robin Isle and...America?"

"No bridge. Horses and buggies come and go on a rope-and-pulley barge. Run four times a day, six days a week, I hear."

"I see."

"Mildred May?"

"Yes, dear?"

"Mighty glad you got yourself into this here boat. No need to be all teary-eyed about what I'm saying. Wait now, them be happy tears, or sad ones? Can't tell nothing about a crying woman!"

I felt like there was some kind of spiky animal holed up in my throat trying to climb out. Thaddeus did not press further, for which I was grateful. He rowed on, in quiet, except for the steady creaking of oarlocks.

As the gap between me and what I had always known widened, I searched for another glimpse of family. All I found was empty beach. My quiet weeping turned into a dull whimper.

"You sure you have the right woman?" I ventured after some time, between humiliating sniffles.

"I do."

"How do you know?"

"Because you are the only one for me."

"You mean I am the only one you want, or the only one you could have?"

"Both."

"I see." I dipped my hand into the ocean. She was calmer than expected, given the winds on Crescent. I could faintly smell my island's shore from the seaweed stains on the dress.

"Got in the boat. Mine now."

"Got in the boat." I agreed to that.

"Popplestone ain't a bad place, Mildred May. Well, north Popplestone's plum full of stuck-up creatures. Down south, though, in Gale—I mean Hale—Harbor, well, it's mighty special. Not perfect. Needs more people. I've told you about it some."

"Yes, you have."

"Best to not talk about it, can see for yourself in about four hours. We'll make good time today pulled out by the tide."

"Thought we left because of the storm."

"Not much of a storm. Riding the ebbing tide, well that be important. We're making three knots now with the current instead of one if against. Four hours of rowing instead of twelve."

I turned to the island that Thaddeus and the current were pulling me away from.

"My, oh my!"

"What?"

"I have never seen Crescent from out to sea. The island is so flat! Lordy, without those spruce trees it would look like a floating pancake, barely visible at all."

"Crescent is a sight bigger than Popplestone."

"Hard to imagine anything smaller than Crescent."

I turned back around and looked forward, past Thaddeus. A deep-purple Popplestone Isle rose high in the distance like a breaching whale.

"Damn good fishing over there, Mildred. And not much competition."

"Why is there no competition?"

"Too hard to live out there."

"I see."

"You'll be fine, big strong woman like you are."

"Well I—"

"Better be! Need babies right quick."

"Please, I...I...could you just keep rowing and not talk about that?"

"Yes, ma'am."

Soon we were more than halfway across the bay.

"Mr. Gale?"

"Keep calling me Thaddeus."

"I have never been this far away from home."

Thaddeus leaned forward, the oars rising out of the water behind him, his knuckles around the ends a few inches from my jacket. He leaned back, setting the oars' blade ends in the water as waves swirled around them, and then pulled again.

Another lean forward and back again before he said, "You're going home Mildred, not leaving it."

"Yes, but—"

"No buts."

"But—"

"Said no buts!"

"Thaddeus, my word, you have never spoken to me like that!"

"You were not my wife before."

"That gives you no right!"

"Oh, but it does."

"Does not."

"We will see about that."

"Yes, we will."

"Can't go back."

I took a deep breath and placed a hand against the inwale, steadying myself. A swell lifted the stern, momentarily placing me higher than Thaddeus. I yelled against the wind, "Not planning to go back! Is just that, well, this is hard, is all!"

The stern dropped, along with my stomach.

"Ain't hard. You're just sitting there."

"When I was nine, my best friend Otto never returned from nearly this very spot during a storm. Otto's father washed ashore a week later covered with some kind of sea maggot. Never found Otto."

"Stop cluttering your mind with the past."

The man extended two long fingers off his right oar and took hold of the white silk ribbon of my jacket. I pulled back, causing it to untie and flap about. Without the jacket, he could see through my dress there.

I hastily retied the bow.

"Concentrate on rowing, Mr. Gale, I beg of you! I want to beat the change of current to shore."

"So do I, my Mrs. Gale, so do I. Spending the night in a boat ain't much of a wedding event now is it? Got to get ourselves home right quick."

I leaned over the rail and retched, leaving breakfast floating upon the sea.

Thaddeus laughed—*he laughed*—as I wiped mouth and chin with my arm.

"Not funny."

"A sight you are!"

"*Not* funny."

"Maybe not now, but someday you'll think so."

"I highly doubt that."

"You always need the last word?"

"No."

"Good. See them islands over there, south of Popplestone? Look at those. Will help settle your stomach."

As the breeze picked up, we climbed, and dipped again, two boats on a deep-blue, moving field. Every dozen or so rolls a bigger wave came through, soaking us with spray. I again let my breakfast fly, half of it blowing back into the peapod and spattering the insides.

"Making a mess of my fishing boat, Mildred."

"I am so sorry."

"Not much of a wedding day for you."

"It's all right. Just sick, is all."

"Weather's turning away. These seas are nothing, I tell you. Have traveled Silver Bay in a whole lot worse. 'Course, not with a lady and loaded boat in tow. Any rougher, we would've had to let her go—the boat, that is, not you."

"Thank you for keeping Pa's dory and my things, Thaddeus."

"You know, Mildred, once I saw a blue whale, the whole shebang of a whale, breaching itself right up, blowing spray, and looking at me with his big old crinkly eye. Nothing more amazing than the sea and her creatures. You respect her, not be stupid, and she'll take care of you."

"That is lovely, Thaddeus."

"Nothing lovely about it. Just the damn straight truth."

As we rowed into Hale Harbor, Thaddeus, big hands resting on the oars, jerked his head to his right, gesturing me to look. A two-story white clapboard home slid into view from the long harbor's western shore.

"My oh my, Thaddeus, your house looks like our wedding cake! Lordy be, how I wish we had not left that whole cake on Crescent."

"Tall cake like that would've slopped all over the boat."

"Such an elegant home. I have never seen anything like it in all my days."

The house possessed the harbor's northwest corner, a turret of windows with its own cone-shaped roof its most striking feature. A porch wrapped around two sides, facing west toward fields and south to the harbor. Ornate posts. Intricate railings. Stately windows.

I noticed four other houses scattered around the harbor.

"Why, everyone can see each other from their homes!"

"Mighty handy in a storm, can look out for one another. Other times, right annoying having some neighbor poking their noses in my business."

"I can well imagine. My oh my...people!"

I fussed with my hair.

"With them lovely fair curls a-dangling, don't need to worry about nothing."

"I am a tad nervous."

"These harbor folks are mostly fine. A few bad apples not contributing enough, but nothing too terrible, except for one."

"The same as on Crescent. Probably the same as all islands."

"Got that right."

"What about the rest of the island?"

"Three other towns. Popplestone uptown be the biggest. Got a store, post office, even a boardinghouse there. Halfway down the island on the east there's Preacher Cove. Hale is the farthest south and smallest by far of the four. Go west from Hale about a mile and a half for Gooseneck. All told, let's see, something a little over two hundred living on the island year-round. A lot more come summers."

"Thank you for the geography lesson. Dare say I will be needing quite a few of those."

"Don't need to know nothing outside of Hale."

"Your house, it is as fine a place as I have ever seen!"

"You will be living more fine than anyone on Crescent."

"That I will. Thank you, Thaddeus."

"Almost home now, made it in good time."

I scanned the open land just beyond the harbor's mudflats. Few trees. Six lived-in houses were all I could see, counting ours and noticing one more tucked away in a wooded patch.

"Everyone is coming to greet us!"

"'Course they are."

"I must look a wreck."

"You look wicked pretty, if you ask me, wedding dress and all. And those oversized rubber boots be a mighty nice touch."

"My boots fit me just fine."

"I see. Sure need them today. Got to walk all the way up in that muck, being low tide and all. Would have liked to arrive at high tide—more convenient for unloading. Would've meant fighting the current all the way here, though."

"I do not mind the walk. Your harbor is beautiful."

"That she is, glad you think so too, Mrs. Gale."

I wiped a couple of tired curls from the front of my face and checked the stain on my sleeve—it was fairly light. I retied the lopsided mess of string holding my jacket together.

"May I borrow your handkerchief?"

Thaddeus paused, held both oars with his left hand, pulled his hanky out of his pocket, and handed it to me.

I wiped my face. "What will they think of me?"

"They think highly of me so they will think highly of my wife."

"That makes me more nervous."

Seven men, young to middle-aged, each wearing knee-high boots like mine and big smiles, waded out. Thaddeus pulled in the oars.

"You made good time," said one.

"Got here a new boat, too."

"And wife!"

"That too."

The men grabbed our laden vessel and ran it to the beach, Thaddeus and I holding onto the rails.

The moment we dragged upon the bottom, several women and two young children swarmed about in the shallow water, helping me out. The dory drifted behind us, tugging at its rope. My boots squashed and slipped in thick, floating amber seaweed, the likes of which I had never smelled so strong. The smallest woman, perhaps in her early twenties, giggled, eyes sparkling shyly under a tattered pale-blue bonnet.

Another petite woman stepped forward as the timid one moved aside.

"Welcome, sister-in-law! I am Mineola Browne, but call me Min. Married to Thaddeus's stepbrother Marvin. Live in that yellow house behind yours."

Mineola smiled wide, tossing thick locks of her dark hair about. "Well now, gracious me, Eve can't brag about being the tallest woman in the harbor no more!"

"So nice to meet you, Min," I replied, wondering why Thaddeus had not told me about a brother.

Min leaned into my ear and whispered, "I don't have any children."

"Why, that is fine, certainly."

"Ain't fine, not here! Must have new children, only four left. Marv and I are still trying, but...well, been ten years now."

I wanted to hug her, but another woman practically shoved Min away.

"I'm Eve Thomas of the green house. Husband Irville is the gangly one there. Two sons Irville Junior and Samuel be around here somewhere. Ten and nine they are. Them boys get rowdy in class, just pretend you are about to smack them. Works for us, and we've never actually had to hit them, thank God."

"I look forward to meeting your boys."

"Here they come."

A small boy and a tall one raced along a path from the pale-green house set back from the harbor. They ran so fast, seemed an imaginary ghost chased them. They jumped onto the beach from a grassy patch and darted toward us in the mud. They arrived breathless, stopping in front of me, hands straight down their sides.

"Welcome," said older brother Irville, still looking at the ground.

"Yes, welcome," agreed Samuel, looking at the same place.

"Why, thank you both, and what handsome young men you are!"

The two looked at each other and then ran off, east along the shore. They flitted left and right, seemingly going nowhere planned and nearly bumping into each other, kicking up beach muck as they ran.

"Boys! Come back here and help unload!"

"Seems I scared them off."

"Aren't used to talking much, except to each other. Boys!"

They raced back and picked a chest up out of the dory.

Nothing could be placed on the wet beach. Loaded up, small and big fellas alike began walking toward the house.

"And you are?" I asked another small woman with long black hair braided neatly behind her back. I felt positively huge compared to these women, just as I always had on Crescent.

"Flora Bell. My husband is that short man wearing overalls, Miles. We live on the farm on the harbor's eastern peninsula."

Flora placed her hands on a young girl's shoulders.

"And here is our daughter, Lucy. She is seven."

Lucy had her father's golden locks, while her oval face resembled Flora's.

"Lucy! How nice to meet you, and your mother. I look forward to getting to know you better, and to having you in my class."

The girl hugged me. *She hugged me!* Her tiny arms barely circled my wide hips.

My heart happily in my throat, I hugged her back and tousled her hair.

"And you, young man?" I asked the last of the children, a boy hovering behind the woman with the bonnet.

"I'm Orris. I be eight. This here is my mom."

"I am Pearl. Pearl Jennings."

The boy continued, "And my...my...pop is there...and the one bringing your anchor up the beach is my brother Jon. Stepbrother. He is sixteen."

"So pleased to meet you both. Which house do you live in?"

Pearl pointed east to a two-story home in need of paint.

"Orris, come help me!" Lucy called. Orris ran to Lucy, and behind me the two children lifted my dress's train out of the mud. They were too late, but I liked their sweet gesture.

At the edge of our property, a tall, middle-aged man with salt-and-pepper hair took my elbow and guided me up three stone steps to a grassy spot in front of our house, Thaddeus by my side, hand on my back.

"Thank you," I said, pausing to appreciate purple and pink lupine weaved into fields of yellow-green behind him.

"My pleasure, Mrs. Gale. Glad you are here safe and sound."

I gave that man a second glance. There was something familiar about him.

"Mildred, you going to just stand there? Come see your house."

"Yes, I would like that, Thaddeus."

"Pick her up," ordered Eve. "She's in her wedding dress, after all!"

And there, in front of the small crowd standing on the shore, the harbor extending far behind them, Thaddeus swooped me up as if I was a mere feather.

I wrapped my arms around his neck, and laughed deep to cheers, whoops, and hollers as he carried me inside.

Outhaul

"Like your kitchen?"

I ran my hand down dark cherry cabinets lining the wall. "Beautiful. And that's quite a cookstove. Oh my, it is a Castle Tucker!"

"And look here at your well pump, also the best. Like the color?"

"I certainly do love red. And I sure will enjoy looking at the beach through that glass window while washing dishes. The woodworking is especially fine."

"Built them cabinets myself, and the wainscot, too."

"Did you eat eggs before you rowed to Crescent?"

"How did you know?"

"I can smell them."

"Glory be, guess you can. Didn't wash out the skillet."

"No matter, I will wash it later."

I reached out and held his hand then, the first time I had ever done so. "Thaddeus, the ivory white of the walls, well, that is my favorite color for inside a home."

"Every room is the same. It's um...well, would you look at that! Is like your dress."

"I practically blend into the wall, except for the mud on my dress."

Thaddeus swept his hand in the direction of a large room with bay windows facing the harbor. "And here is the living room. See them pine boards? They reach all the way across the floor, not a one cut shorter along the way."

"This is all so beautiful, Thaddeus. How long did it take to build?"

"A year. Built the barn first so I'd have a workshop, and then the house. Put it all up near the end of the Knickerbocker mess. Nobody else constructing much around here, so got myself a good price on materials. First of springtime four years ago, captain of the *Mary E* brought the whole shipment of lumber right to the wharf, unloading it along with four nicely underpaid men to help me build it. 'Course I designed her, but an architect from Portland put his plans to it so we builders wouldn't mess it up. Which we didn't, clearly."

"Clearly."

Mineola popped her head in the door. "Should we bring in the luggage? Don't want to interrupt any smooching going on now!"

I dropped his hand.

"Bring it all right into my living room," bellowed Thaddeus, arms opening wide.

My new neighbors entered the house in hasty fashion, boots clomping, arms full of suitcases and boxes. The smallest boy, Orris, noticed mud trailing his wet shoes, took them off and left them on the porch.

"This is as gorgeous as Marv said!" Min exclaimed.

"I'll say!" Pearl caressed the trim around the first bay window and then pulled her hand back abruptly, as if it was too nice to touch.

Eve looked about, mouth open, and whistled.

"Got to fill this up with children, lots of them." Eve looked at Min, who scowled.

Flora glanced about the room. "Elegant."

Flora's husband, Miles, followed her gaze. "Sure is."

"Well, don't just stand there gawking. Got me a wife here now!"

The visitors scattered except for Thaddeus's stepbrother, Marv. That wisp of a woman, Pearl, giggled again, hand covering her mouth as she ran out.

"Would have been fine if they had stayed, dear."

"They was all figuring what I spent, about ready to cackle about it. And I spent a lot less than they'd be guessing. Not stupid with money."

"They have never seen the inside of your home in all these years?"

"Nope. Just Marvin here, and Irville. They come over for...for you know, chatting."

"Chatting?"

"Chatting."

"Yes, chatting." Marv nodded.

"Why are you still hanging around here, Marv?"

"Just to say don't worry about those boats stuck on the flats. I'll come down every few hours and move the anchor up until tide's high enough for me to put them on the outhaul."

"Obliged. Got a bride here."

"Best I be off then. Welcome again, Mrs. Gale."

"Thank you for everything, Mr. Browne.

"Call me Marv."

"Then call me Mildred. We are kin, after all."

"That we are. So glad to know you."

Marv left us surrounded by boxes and trunks.

"Best we unpack." I picked up a box.

"Unpacking can wait."

"But I cannot wait to... My oh my, I need the outhouse rather desperately!"

"In the barn. Pee pot upstairs. Take your pick. And I'll be needing an early supper. You be needing it, too, after everything you lost on the way."

My arms froze up first, and then they felt like rubber. I suddenly missed my little brothers, who did not care what kind of meal I put in front of them as long as there was a lot of it.

"Don't you worry about nothing," said Thaddeus, perhaps noticing my furrowed brow. "The girls left a casserole and more when they came in, didn't you see that?"

"That is so kind of them, first day and all."

"Another benefit of marrying—got some free grub out of it."

I glanced about the kitchen, a larger room than the living room. The kitchen doorway stepped right out onto the porch.

Just then, that darling little Lucy, the youngest of the harbor, darted back inside, screen door slamming behind her.

She took my hand in hers. "I hope you like it here. Not like the others. We all want you to stay, is already decided."

The girl had one blue eye and one brown.

Lucy dropped my hands and ran out of the house before I could think of a reply. She jumped the full length of stairs onto the grass and raced after her parents.

"Mildred? MILDRED MAY!"

"Yes, Thaddeus!"

"Hungry! Been rowing all the hell afternoon, for Christ's sake."

"Yes, Thaddeus!"

I found the casserole and raised the yellow metal lid, delighting in the steam curling up from melted cheese oozing over chunks of fish. The dish smelled strongly of rosemary.

I put the top back on and dashed upstairs to use the pink-flowered pee pot. Thaddeus ran to the outhouse in the barn.

"Got a confession."

Thaddeus sat on the foot of our four-poster mahogany bed, feet on the floor, legs so long his knees rose above the mattress. Must have been nearly nine o'clock by the time we finished supper and unpacked some.

I faced my new husband, my back against the window, wearing a pink nightie under a faded peach housecoat Mama had given me.

A beautiful night, and I felt better than expected, fortified perhaps by a rich meal. The evening's full moon fashioned a path of flickering silver-white light on the flat black sea of the harbor.

"Confession? What is it, my dear?"

A long pause before he replied, "This will be my first time."

Thaddeus's thumbs twitched.

"Everything works you know. Know that…I just, well, you can see around here, not too many women. Not those kind. Not that I'd go that way. Just not all sure how to do right…by you, especially your first time. Ah…*our* first time. Would you say something so I can stop talking?"

"Maybe we can wait?"

"Been waiting since eleven years old, for Christ's sake, not waiting no more!"

"Okay. We are married. We have to."

"Not supposed to be a chore."

"Not a chore. I am nervous too, truth be told."

"Understand that...um...do you ever think about things? Could start there."

"No."

"Oh."

"Yes...actually yes."

Thaddeus stood up. "What have you thought about?"

I took a step toward him.

"Well, things."

"Things?"

"Little things."

"Such as?"

"A kiss...not a peck, a real smooch, soft and long and slow."

As I whispered my wishes, I felt a strange and comforting warmth spread through me, building in some areas more than others. *Comes naturally, you'll see...* Ma's words echoed again in my ears.

Thaddeus placed his large weathered hands on my shoulders. I was pleased to feel nothing but trust.

"Cap."

Thaddeus pulled off his plain brown hat. "Let me try. I *have* kissed before."

"Okay."

I closed my eyes. And waited.

And waited.

Waited yet more.

I opened my eyes. Thaddeus's hands were still on my shoulders, but he looked beyond me, squinting at the middle of our sparkling harbor.

"Glory be, herring are running! Irville and Marvin better be getting their arses down here mighty quick!"

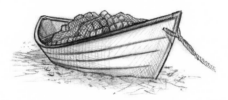

"Go Thaddeus, go!"

I clambered down the stairs on his boot heels, as excited as those fish, my housecoat flapping open. Thaddeus pulled up his dark-brown suspenders as he ran. He looked good. I was proud.

"Glad my weir is ready. But we've got to work fast to get them ends netted off or we won't have a pot to piss in!"

While we rushed through the house, Irville and Marvin pulled on the outhaul to bring in two dories heaped with thick netting. They leaned backwards as they strained to secure the laden boats, as if slowly winning at tug-of-war.

I stuffed three plump biscuits into Thaddeus's shirt before he shot out the door.

"You'll have to wait, my Mildred! Hope I'm worth it to you, girl."

"You are! You are!" I replied from the porch, silently thanking those fish for giving me more time before going beyond kissing.

I tied my housecoat up tight. Thaddeus barked his orders.

The harbor was so full of blue-backed silver herring, some jumped out of the water and were left gasping for breath on the beach.

"My word!" I said to nobody in particular.

"You'd be talking to yourself except I'm here to hear you."

"Min!"

She had come up the steps at the back end of the porch. Hastily dressed, my sister-in-law wore a green waist-length sweater over a white nightgown.

"In all my years on Crescent, I have never seen such a run!"

"Let's catch us some, what do you say?"

"Let's!"

I grabbed two baskets hanging from the porch rafters and followed Mineola to the beach. Laughing, she lifted up her nightie, the moonlight illuminating absolutely everything else through the fine cloth. I grabbed a cold, slimy fish with two hands, placing it in my basket, where it flopped about.

"You know," Min said as a fish flew out of her hands, landed on a rock, and then wiggled itself into the water, "this much herring means a whole mess of loot! And all the bait needed for the rest of the season."

"No wonder the men are working at a frenetic pace."

"Frenetic?"

"Yes, frenetic, um...fast."

"You sure use some big words, teacher."

"Sorry."

"No need. As long as you ain't uppity about it."

"Would never!"

"Then use all the big words you like."

Dozens of writhing bait fish spilled onto the sandy part of the beach just below the highest tide mark. A few pogies mixed with the herring.

"Something's chasing them," Min offered. "Seals probably."

"A predator could send them right back out of the harbor."

"Mildred's right."

"Eve!"

"Our boys, look at them go!"

As the harbor filled with fish, our fellas scrambled to stop their escape.

Min bit her lip. "Uh-oh, here come the interlopers. Our boys are not going to like that."

I followed Min's gaze to Leroy Jennings, with his older son Jon and neighbor Rufus Mank, dragging his boat to the harbor. The men groaned as they pulled the heavy vessel out, its keel marking a thick line in the mud. "Surely, there are plenty of fish to go around. My goodness, there are *too* many."

Eve added, "Won't stop Irv, Marv, and Thaddeus pissing in the water to mark their territory."

Min swatted Eve on the shoulder. "The mouth on you, girl!"

"Just telling it the way it is."

I looked out at the sea. "We are all of the same harbor, why not get along?"

Min threw a stone into the water. "I know, my dear, don't make no sense. Just is."

Eve pointed to their boats. "Well, would you look at our fellas now."

The men closed the gap on the western side, which would help direct the fish into a funnel to their capture. As they secured the last string of netting along a post at the far end of the weir, the three looked our way.

We responded with waves, cheers, and whistles.

Instead of rowing to the eastern side to prevent a reverse direction escape, our boys headed toward the interlopers' boat.

Two boats. Six men standing, the ones in the middle rowing forward. Heading straight for each other across an agitated bay.

"This ain't going to be good," Mineola moaned.

Seconds later, boats collided, planks scraping as they nearly slid right by each other. Off balance, arms a-flailing, the men grabbed each other across the water to stop the boats. I could not make out the words through the yelling. Eve, Min, and I glared, hands on our hips.

After more shouting and gesturing, then talking more regular-like, they headed toward the eastern gap.

"They are working together!" Pearl appeared by our side, clapping.

Eve wrapped her arm around Pearl's shoulder. "By the grace of God, you're right. Now that's a scene to behold."

"Have to," said Min. "These fish won't stay long. See there? Some are jumping straight up out of the water!"

Eve let out a deep breath. "Damn seals."

"Biscuits and jam, girls?"

Min nodded and turned to the house. "That would be divine, Mildred. Made them myself, and they are some good."

I followed her. "The boys have your biscuits, too. You gals sure gave me a fine welcome. I could not imagine cooking my first night here. Thank you."

As we ate on the porch, we watched our fellas and Rufus race against the school's next move by moonlight, looking out to sea as if watching one of those newfangled black-and-white films. The men looked like puppets, lively black silhouettes along the dark-sea horizon. Only our movie had sound—Thaddeus snapping orders, the rush of boats, the grinding of oars turning in metal oarlocks, fish jumping and splashing, and thick nets dropping into the churning sea.

"So, Mildred, if you don't mind me asking, have you and Thaddeus—"

Mineola shook her head. "Leave her be, Eve."

"We've got to have more babies around here."

"First night. Not even half a night. Give her time."

"Don't got ten years."

"Please!" I begged. "Can we not talk about this?"

"All right," replied Eve, "but we need more young'uns right quick, that's for sure."

Near on eleven o'clock, and every Hale resident was on the beach, in a boat, or on my porch. Todd Calderwood, the fellow with graying hair, and Flora Bell's husband, Miles, chatted while they watched the working men. Flora and daughter Lucy, Eve's two sons, Irv and Sam, and Pearl's young Orris hung close to the shore, too. The children squealed as they captured grounded fish then hurled them into the harbor to see who could throw the farthest.

⁂

Finally, and just in time, Thaddeus, Marvin, and Irville slid their boat alongside Rufus and the two Jenningses, having closed the final gap together.

"A miracle!" Min exclaimed, as we watched the six men, three in each vessel, reach across the water to shake hands.

"The fish are trying to get out!" Pearl jumped up and down.

"Pearl is right!" Eve put her hands on her head as she watched, mouth agape. "Look at them go!"

As herring plowed into the cod-end netting from the weir's funnel, it filled up into a tight, pulsating ball, a few lucky fish spilling out as the men cinched the net.

"Going to be a long night," said Eve. "They'll be lugging them fish to shore so they're not supper for seals, sharks, and porpoises. Got to be a ton of fish we got there. Never seen this much caught in one night or day. You brought a pot of luck to us, Mildred."

"Eve's right. And we're glad you are here, fish or no fish." Min took my hand.

I squeezed hers back. "Will they have enough salt to preserve them?"

Min smiled. "Thaddeus will, and they'll put a lot of them in the lobster pound. He's always well prepared, your fella, that and buying the best boats makes us all successful. Just as long as it don't got a sail on her, or nothing newfangled mechanical."

"Thaddeus doesn't like sailing?" Flora asked.

Min continued, "Thaddeus tried sailing once. Didn't take, will leave it at that. He won't go for new Make 'N Breaks from New Hampshire, neither. What does he say? 'Not going to buy anything for the sea from a Hampster!' Yes, that's what he says, don't think they'd know anything about the sea, being so far inland and all."

"Well, Portsmouth, New Hampshire is on the coast."

"Mildred is correct, it is." Flora nodded.

Eve, Min, and Pearl stared at Flora and me blankly.

"You don't know New Hampshire borders the Atlantic?" I knew I was showing off.

"Well now, are you sure?"

"Yes, I am sure. I am surprised you all don't know that."

"Well, no need to be so uppity."

Min waved her hand in our faces and frowned. "Portsmouth, who cares where it is. Hale is the place! Your fella's darn good for this here harbor. And you being here is 'cuz of him. Tonight, we just all got rich, for a little while anyway. Things going to be better now."

Little Lucy's words floated back to me then: *I hope you like it here. Not like the others.*

Deep into that first night on Popplestone Isle, I lit the oil lamp over the extra-wide sink and then moved to the door, watching Thaddeus single-handedly haul the peapod high off the beach before coming inside.

"Evening, Mildred."

"More like morning, Mr. Gale." I wiped my hands on my apron. "The sun will be rising in a few hours."

"You stayed up."

"I did."

"For me."

"For you."

Thaddeus walked by me and washed his hands in the white porcelain bowl, silent. He took a soapy brown sponge to his neck. I turned my back to give him privacy. I heard him squeeze out the sponge then plunge it back in the water. I sensed him unbuttoning that blue shirt of his, my favorite color on him. That shirt fell to the floor with several *clinks* as the metal buttons hit the wooden surface, followed by the louder *thwonk* of his suspender clips and what they held up.

I moved to the window, the night sky looking so close felt like I could handpick one of those giant sparkling stars out for my very own.

Thaddeus came up behind me, his hand drifting down my back, gently tugging on my pale-yellow blouse. He reached around my midriff with two hands and slowly unbuttoned my shirt from the bottom up. His hands behind me again, he loosened the tiny knot of my apron, which then drifted to the floor. I counted the larger stars, not moving, not speaking.

He reached around to my front again and then down, resting his hand there, in that private place.

"This all right, what I am doing?"

"Yes."

With Thaddeus's right cheek nestled in my hair, his right hand still resting below my stomach, he snuggled his other hand inside my opened blouse and held me there, over my brassiere.

"This still all right?"

"Yes."

We stayed that way for some time before moving up to the bedroom in the turret.

Later that morning, I lay in bed feeling better than I could ever remember, listening to tiny waves collapsing along the shore as if tired from their long journeys.

I sat up and stretched my arms. It was foggy outside, but I felt clear.

"Ah, look at you two," I whispered through the window. Could just see a pair of great blue herons in the mist, one extra-large, the female.

"Good luck fishing to you, Mrs. and Mr. Heron."

I put on the white lace intimates Ma had placed in my suitcase with a wink, the same yellow blouse I'd worn the evening before, and pulled on my light-blue skirt that tied under my bosom with a navy ribbon. I went downstairs, sliding my left hand on the smooth mahogany railing, a banister so grand I felt like the Queen of England touching it.

I found Thaddeus sitting outside on the porch steps, head in his hands.

I sat down, put my arm around him, and rested my head on his shoulder.

"What is the matter, Thaddeus?"

My head bounced as he looked up and yelled, "What's the matter is that...well, seems I sort of love you, Mildred. Just didn't wager on that!"

My right hand dropped as he stood. I watched his hunched back as he stomped to the barn amidst fog wafting out of the harbor.

"Goddamn son of a bitch!"

I jumped to my feet.

"Going to kill that son of a bitch!"

Through wisps of white, I could barely see the outline of a rowboat in the middle of the harbor, a man standing in its center holding something.

"Is someone hauling your traps?"

"Damn right!"

"My oh my."

The man who had just professed his love to me barked, "More than 'my oh my,' woman!"

"Please do not hurt him. Looks like Jon. He is just a boy."

"A boy stealing."

I stared, not believing my eyes. It was Jon! "But Thaddeus, surely someone made him do it!"

"Stealing is stealing. Go back inside where you can be useful."

As I went inside, I prayed with all my might he would not actually kill the boy. Thaddeus continued to curse as he dragged the peapod to the water.

North Haven island's Omar Thomas was awarded
a square lobster trap patent on September 20, 1888.

I grabbed a biscuit and sat on the porch. I could not see much, but voices travel through fog louder than anything.

"Mr. Gale!" Jon cried.

A splash. A trap must have dropped overboard.

Thaddeus growled like a wolf.

"Mr. Gale, I—"

"What are you doing, you damn thieving fool?" Thaddeus roared.

"Nothing, I...was just looking."

"Looking, are you? What's them lobsters doing here?"

I imagined lobsters in Jon's boat, crawling backwards and in circles, claws poised to strike each other.

"Cat got your tongue? Them bugs yours?"

"Yes, sir?"

"*Not* yours."

Boats bumped with hollow thuds. Sounded like a trap dropped into the hull of one of them.

"You touch my gear again, you won't be so lucky. Want your chopped-up body in my pots, feeding my harbor lobsters? See you out here again messing with my stuff, you won't see another day. Got it?"

Did not hear Jon's reply. Perhaps he nodded.

"Good lad. Got the message, I see."

As Thaddeus rowed inland out of the fog, I yelled, "He is just a boy!"

"Shush up, Mildred, the whole neighborhood can hear you."

I spoke louder, even though by then he was right in front of me. "Will tell the world, I will!"

"You leave the fishing business to me, woman," he snarled, climbing out of the boat. "Don't you have lessons to start? That's a mighty important job around here, you know. Is why I..."

"Is why you what?"

"Nothing."

"He's a boy."

"Sixteen ain't no boy on Popplestone. You know damn well I started fishing at twelve. 'Course, he did pee his own self. Guess he don't have a real man's courage yet."

"A boy," I repeated, pained that Thaddeus had scared Jon so badly he wet himself.

"If he's doing a man's work, he's a man, can't treat him no different. Fishing decisions are mine, I tell you. Go fix me breakfast while I hitch up the boat."

"Just a boy! Sent out to do his father's bidding in the fog!"

"Keep your head on the home and school, am warning you, Mildred."

"Warning me?"

"That's right."

I was about to tell him to go piss on the edge of the shore so I would know where not to tread, but his eyes, dark as coffee beans, stopped me.

"Sounds like you need a good breakfast to get you back in a right mood."

"A sight better, Mrs. Gale."

I slammed the teapot on the stove and felt a piece of me slip away.

11

Traps with curved tops overlapped and followed square wooden trap use. Arthur A. Noyes was awarded a curved-top, folding lobster trap patent on November 25, 1913.

The July days of 1912 melded together, most of them so sticky-hot even the sea seemed to slow up as she lumbered in. Thaddeus had been showing me the chores: cleaning, cooking his favorites, laundry, tending the chickens, house painting, and more. I washed salt off the windows, dusted the tiny grooves in the wainscot, polished brass hardware hinges on cabinet doors, and boiled water for his baths. There was a precise time and way to do everything according to Mr. Gale, including weekly emptying of the outhouse, a task I desperately despised. I resigned myself to his needs, telling myself they were mine, too. They were, for the most part. And it was my house, too. And yet I pined away for more, something all and only for me.

Our stately home needed softness and privacy, so I sewed up white lace curtains, five sets a week, until complete. I started with the bedroom, where the busy world faded away. He was gentle there our first summer, a contrast to his often gruff exterior first thing in the mornings.

Another favorite place was sitting at our little table in the kitchen looking over the harbor come suppertime, for it was then we chatted, learning more about each other. Good food tempered Thaddeus, while strong workdays relaxed him some.

"How did you get all this done while you fished?" I asked one evening after we had devoured a herring, cheese, rosemary, and potato omelet.

"Not easy. Did it."

"You could still do a few chores. Like the outhouse."

"That be yours."

"I will be teaching in the fall, full-time work, same as you."

"The house is your responsibility, Mildred, is why I..."

"Why you what?"

"Never you mind. Just get your jobs done."

"I will do my best. I just think it is too much."

"Doing your best is probably good enough."

"It does not seem fair."

"What's not fair?"

"There is so much to do! All me? What about you?"

"I fish."

"But I do everything else. Everything!"

"I paid for this here house."

"You mean I am working as an indentured servant to pay it back?"

"What?"

"I scrub the stench of rancid fish bait off your clothes every day! That, after cleaning, cooking, doing other laundry, the chickens, sewing, on and on."

"Glory be, woman, every fisherman's wife washes and mends her husband's clothes."

"I feel like a slave."

"Ain't so."

"It is how I feel."

"But you ain't a slave, just a wife."

"Then take care of the outhouse, like you did before I arrived. And do your own straightening up of the workshop and shed, at least."

Thaddeus let out a sigh. "All right, I'll do that, but sometimes fishing days are long so that we can pay for everything we have."

"I understand."

"This was some fine meal, Mildred. I appreciate you, am telling you straight."

"Thank you, Thaddeus, glad for it."

12

I finally wrote to Ma end of July. I told her all about Hale Harbor life, how it was different, and how it was the same, as on Crescent. I described my neighbors, especially the youngsters, that Min and I were sisters-in-law, how I looked forward to teaching in the fall, the exciting herring run and Thaddeus's successful lobster fishing.

I also bragged about our grand house, that we had chickens, and that Thaddeus owned a pile of land on the west side of the harbor. Truth be told, I hoped she would be envious, at least a little bit.

I asked Ma to hug everyone. And I begged her to bring Julia to Popplestone for a visit.

I carefully folded the letter, put it in an envelope, glued it shut, and wrote, as neatly as I could to impress the Popplestone and Crescent postmistresses:

Mrs. Meredith Combs
Crescent Island, Maine

I placed the envelope on the counter and went downstairs to fix supper, feeling well-accomplished and even important. I had never written a letter sent by official post!

Thaddeus slathered up a roll with butter. "Mildred May?"

"Yes?"

"You happy here?"

He dunked the roll into a crock of beans, soaking up the juice.

"What kind of question is that?"

"Mine."

"Yes, I am happy enough."

"A little one underfoot would make you happier."

"I suppose so."

"I know so. Would make me, ah, even happier, too."

"We would be mighty busy, with you fishing, and me teaching, and all the chores, having a baby, too."

"We'd make do."

"I suppose so."

"I know so."

"We can have a child, certainly, dear."

"Good. Mighty good."

"Thaddeus?"

"Yes?"

"Tell me more about the sea."

"She's hard to describe."

"Try."

"Well, she's fickle, never the same, not even one day the same, not ever. Look at her now. Even after a bright day of sun, she's turned dark gray in just an hour. Her colors, they can be all sorts of blue and grays and even black, and sometimes so light she is almost white. Don't ever cross the sea none, or she'll claim you for her own forever."

"On Crescent, we lost some good men, and...even boys. And once, a woman."

"They're all stupid."

"They were unlucky."

"No such thing as an accident on the sea. A man's got to read her mood, not go out if she ain't looking or feeling right by him."

"That does not seem fair. Weather can change suddenly. Nobody can anticipate every possibility."

"I can. And I'm always right about the sea. Am usually right about other things, too."

"Always?"

"Always about the sea."

"What about our house?"

"What about it?"

"Are we safe here in a really big storm?"

"Only storms worth worrying about in Hale are straight-on southerlies. Them gales come barreling into the harbor like a runaway locomotive. If we're in a southerly, hang onto the washing line when you go to the barn shitter so you don't get lost in the squall. Especially in the winter."

"Do you have to say that word?"

"Shitter is what it is."

"You can say outhouse."

"Outhouse, then."

"I think I would hold it during a storm."

"Don't think about storms, Mildred, just prepare for them when you know they be coming. The sea brings gifts, too, you know."

"Lobster, clams, mussels, and fish?"

"Even more. Special gifts."

"Tell me."

"Once, a baby whale found its way into the harbor, seemed to be lost. Marv and Irv, well, they be jumping in the boat with spears and rope! Don't know why at the time, but I didn't join them. Just didn't have the heart for it, I guess. Then the mother called with a high-pitched whistle. The baby clicked back and the mama came raging in, water flying up on both sides of her. The mum and little one, well, they be frantic! Such a good mother she was! She outsmarted them boys, putting herself between her baby and the men, pushing the little one away while giving the water next to the boat a wild swat. Waves swelled up from under her tail and pushed their skiff back and almost over, giving them a mighty ride and the scare of a lifetime. Sure glad about it, too! Was a gift watching her steam out of the harbor with her calf, leaving them boys screaming and waving on a runaway skiff. Gave me quite a chuckle, I tell you! The meat and oil would've been nice, but can't be too greedy about what the sea gives you."

"What a delightful story!"

"I love this harbor, Mildred. More than anything. I hope you do, too."

"I do. Especially its abundance. I have never seen so many clams and mussels in one place. And the snails! We could eat for months here on nothing but what comes from the land and sea if we had to."

"You be right there, Mrs. Gale."

We talked about how the sea is a beauty like no other while we watched the sky glow red as the sun went down, and then the dark sea turned into a stunning turquoise blue, and then black as the early night.

"Thaddeus? Why so fast this time?"

"No time to waste, Mildred."

"But—"

"No buts. This is a job now."

"A job?"

"Got to make that baby."

"That baby?"

"That baby. Our baby. Your baby."

"We could make a baby and still enjoy it."

"I enjoy it. Don't you?"

"You really want me to answer that?"

"I do."

"Then no."

"No?"

"No. I do not enjoy you going so fast."

"Fast. Slow. Don't matter none. Either way makes a baby, may as well be fast about it."

"But—"

"I don't like that word, Mildred, told you that long time ago!"

"Thaddeus..."

"Yes?"

"I need to be loved."

A grunt.

"Here, in bed. Loved."

"I will think about that. Just too tired now."

The man rolled over and went to sleep.

We did not speak again until after supper the next day. He went upstairs right after slurping down a bowl of chowder, holding the bowl to his mouth instead of using a spoon, much of it dribbling down his chin.

Within minutes he returned with a demand. "What's this?"

He held my letter to Ma high in his right hand, the ripped-open envelope in his left. I put down the dish I was washing.

"My letter."

"Not sending it."

"What?"

"Stamp's a waste of money. And this here is too personal."

"Stamps are two cents."

"I work hard for two cents."

"My word, Thaddeus, we have plenty from the herring run. Two pennies! That's one-fifth the price of one little lobster! I will pay you back when I start teaching."

"Not sending it."

"What did I say that was bad?"

"Lots of writing."

I stood up. "What are you talking about?"

"Must be mighty personal, look at all this writing! Who's it to?"

"You did not read it? Why, it's to my mother."

He threw the paper and envelope to the ground, kicking the letter just before it landed on the floor.

Then he pushed me into the wall as he ran by, into the living room and up the stairs.

He pushed me! And kicked my letter! Hurt and angry, I stepped outside onto the porch to be farther away from that man, only to be bitten on the neck by a deer fly. I swatted the insect and cursed,

"Goddamn it!"

"Mildred, you all right?"

"Mr. Calderwood." I looked at Todd and then my hand, insect blood smeared across two fingers.

"Please call me Todd."

He walked in my direction from the beach as I went toward him, wiping my fingers on the back of my apron.

"I am fine, Todd."

"That's good. We are all so glad you're here, Mildred. A special summer for Hale with a new addition."

"I am not too far from away?"

"Certainly not! Need new blood here. Especially one that is so nice."

"You hardly know me. Maybe I am not so nice. You may have just heard me swear, I fear."

"Indeed I did."

"I apologize. I was swearing at a fly, who deemed it necessary to suck the harbor's new blood."

"You are funny, too."

"Sometimes. I hope I am not a joke."

"Mildred, you are not a joke. You are caring. And you will be our children's teacher. How fortunate for them, and for our harbor's parents. For all of us, really. Children are everything for a place like Hale."

"Do you have any?" I blurted out, immediately sorry for falling into such a personal question, given that none lived with him.

"Regrettably, no. I would like a son or daughter, though. Someday maybe."

"Someday, yes I hope so."

"I best be going. Please let me know if you need anything at all." He paused. "Mildred?"

"I am thinking."

"I can wait for you."

"Thaddeus kicked a letter I wrote to my ma." I raised my hand to my mouth, horrified by the personal nature of my revelation.

"Kicked?"

"Yes, it dropped to the floor. He kicked the paper as it went down."

"I see. That's odd."

"It is. I do not understand why."

"What else did he do? What did he say?"

I told Todd everything except the part about Thaddeus shoving me. "Please do not tell anyone what I just said, Todd. I doubt Thaddeus would appreciate me sharing a personal moment like this."

"Certainly."

"What do you make of it?"

"Perhaps Thaddeus can't read. Now and then, children grow up without reading. Is not so uncommon out here, you know, even today. When boys become men, it is too late, and they spend a lifetime trying to hide not being able to."

"That is heartbreaking."

"It is."

"Have you ever seen Thaddeus read anything?"

"Now that I think of it, years ago folks from town distributed an announcement about a meeting in the Popplestone church. I saw your Thaddeus look at it...um...rather blankly. I thought nothing of it at the time. In the context you are sharing, well maybe he could not read it."

"I believe you are right, that he does not read. He asked me where to sign his name on our marriage certificate. His signature was rather basic."

"There is no shame in not being able to read or write."

"Indeed, no shame at all."

"You are a teacher, maybe you can help him."

"I will if I can."

Todd placed his hand on my shoulder and nodded.

"Thank you, Todd. And please drop by again when it suits."

"I would like that, Mildred."

13

"I can help, you know," I said as softly as I could muster, setting a precious piece of chocolate on Thaddeus's pillow as he lay in bed.

"Not sending the letter."

"Never mind about the letter, it is gone." I felt a sharp pang of regret for the first fib to my husband.

"Good."

"I am a teacher, remember?"

"I know that."

"I can teach you to read."

"In your school?"

"No. Here, at home. In private."

He popped the chocolate into his mouth. Sucked on it, not looking up.

"Am sorry for what I done, pushing you like that, ain't one bit right."

"Thank you, Thaddeus. Do not do it again."

"Won't."

"Okay then, reading lesson every Sunday?"

"Every Sunday."

"Good."

"Mighty obliged to you about that."

I lay down next to him.

Nothing fast that night. As he moved slow and well, my mind and body were coaxed back to our first early morning together. I should not have, but I forgave him for the push.

14

"Thaddeus," I said the next morning, "I shall have the mothers over this afternoon."

"What for?"

"To learn more about their children. So that I can do the best I can to teach them come fall."

"So, you'd have all the women over except Min. How do you think she'll feel about that?"

"She would feel terrible! Thank you, Thaddeus. I will fix that."

"Too late."

"Too late?"

"Marv told me about your little get-together yesterday. He said Min's pained up by it."

"Oh dear."

"Small harbor, you know."

"Yes. I should have known better. I was just trying to have a little meeting about school. Min's not—"

"Nope, she ain't no mother, but she still got feelings."

"I will go up there straightaway and apologize."

"Get chores done first."

"I will, Thaddeus."

An hour later, I could stand it no longer and headed for Min's house, chores unfinished.

"Min, may I come in?"

"What for?"

"To apologize."

"You've done nothing wrong."

"You know very well I have. Please Min, let me in. I was a damn fool!"

"I am the damn fool, no children of my own, thinking I could be a real part of this community."

"Min, my word, please, I am begging you. You are everything."

"No children. No job. No nothing."

"I...I cannot stay long. I have so many chores to do. Please come by the house this afternoon around three o'clock."

"But I'm not a mother."

"You are more than a mother. I will reveal just how valuable you are when you come by."

15

A few hours later, Hale's three mothers and I sat on the corner of our porch facing the sea, a gentle breeze keeping mosquitoes at bay. An August afternoon, I had lived in the harbor just over two months. We watched Marvin, Irville, and Thaddeus hauling pots by that wretched ledge schooner captains complained so much about, white froth knocking their vessel about like a cork splashed in a tub.

"Your coffee smells divine!"

"Why, thank you, Flora. I use my mama's recipe."

"Her secret?"

"Grind beans in small batches, percolate fifteen percent more coffee grounds than is typical, and then cook just a wee bit longer. Donut?"

My plate was laden with small, perfectly round donuts, every one of them different: chocolate with coconut flakes, vanilla with a light glaze, cinnamon with sprinkles of brown sugar, and plain ones, too. Flo, Eve, and Pearl helped themselves.

"Flora, may I start with you?"

"Yes?"

"Tell me about Lucy."

"Ahh, Lucy...my goodness, well, she beats to her own drummer. We are still trying to figure out what that beat is so we can try to keep up with her. She is far smarter than Miles or me. Anything she reads, well, it is imprinted on her mind forever."

"A perfect learner."

"Lucy teaches my Orris about things," added Pearl.

Flo sat up straight as she faced Pearl. "Really? What kind of things?"

"The other day, she found five different kinds of spiders. Most ugly spiders!"

"What did she do with them?"

"She told Orris every one of them have eight eyes."

"What kind of girl would notice something like that?" demanded Eve.

"A smart, curious girl," I said. "She is a scientist."

"Well, my Irv and Sam aren't like Lucy at all. They squash spiders any chance they get."

"Orris catches house spiders now. Puts them outside his window. To save them."

"So you're saying Orris is kinder than my boys?"

"Eve, no, not saying that!"

"I'm just messing with you, Pearl, you know that. Orris is a sweet boy, far sweeter than my two."

"Your boys are sweet." Pearl put down her tea.

I searched the road for Min. We sat in the corner of the porch right in her line of sight to the water. She had to be watching us.

Eve took a lot of cream and sugar in her coffee, fiddled with her cup, stirring its contents. "I suppose you'd like to know something about my boys."

"I do."

"Ah, well then, Irville and Samuel, complete brothers."

"Certainly so."

"Not much to say. Just usual boys, I guess, getting into things dirty like that there swamp beyond the house."

"Exploring is good."

"Not when you have laundry to do day in and day out. I keep asking my husband to get me a Hurley machine drum. He won't spend the money. You can't imagine how much laundry there is with those two boys of mine."

"Nobody out here has a Hurley drum," said Flo.

"Only one or two on Crescent have one, that I know of," I added.

"I will never have one." Pearl giggled.

"How long have you lived here, Eve?" I asked.

"Oh, let's see, we have been here, it seems, forever. I was born uptown. Am an Eaton, Evelyn Eaton, a mighty pretty name, but then I became a Thomas about eleven years ago. Sons came not too long after that. Irville Senior's been here all his life. We live in his parents' house."

"His father was a fisherman?"

"Yes. Irville became his only child. His ma and baby brother both died in childbirth when Irville was seven."

Flo and Pearl stared into their cups.

"How horrid!"

"Irv only told me once, his voice cracking like a little boy's. He don't talk about it none. He don't like me talking about it, neither. The girls here know to say nothing about it."

"I understand, Eve. I will not talk about it, not even to Thaddeus."

"Such a shame," Flo added as the rest of us nodded.

"What do you hope for, for your sons in school?"

"To get them out of the house, I bet!" A voice from behind me.

"Mineola!"

Min pulled up a chair. "Give me a cup of that coffee and a chocolate donut."

I smiled at my sister-in-law as I poured coffee in the empty cup. She grinned back, her hair blowing gently about her face.

"Min's right. My boys be destined for fishing, don't see no need for all this highfalutin education. Not like they be going anywhere but straight out there."

Eve pointed to the harbor, its water sparkling in the summer sun. A dozen drifting black guillemots fluttered their wings as waves passed underneath them.

"Well, Miles and I certainly want Lucy to learn more in school."

"Don't know about my Orris. He has to fish, too."

I glanced from mother to mother. "I aim to instill a love of learning and problem solving in the children. That way, they run into something, anything, like a paper from one of these big ships they need to read to get the best price for something, or maybe somebody threatens them, and they understand the law a bit and that the person has no right to threaten...those kinds of things. Would any of this be useful?"

Pearl nodded her head furiously, eyes alight.

Flora clapped her hands. "Absolutely."

"Would indeed," Eve agreed. "Glad now the school won't close up."

I looked at Eve. "Why would it close?"

"You didn't know?"

"Know what?"

"Well, I assumed you knew, is why you came...partly...I mean, at this time..."

"Eve, you are entirely confusing me."

"Tell her, Min. You understand it best."

"All right, I will. You see, Mildred, last year the State of Maine in all its smarts appointed a director to keep an eye on all the 'unorganized territories'—that's what they called us. 'Course we *are* unorganized, but didn't make us feel good to be called that. Anyway, the man came down to Hale one day, saw there weren't no teacher here, said he was going to 'consolidate' unless we got ourselves a real teacher within a year. Close down the Hale Harbor schoolhouse forever! And those no-good, penny-pinching Popplestone uptowners agreed with that cockamamie idea for the taxes they'd save."

"I had no idea!"

"Need ten children to reopen," continued Min. "Who in their right mind would move somewhere with their children where there's no schoolhouse...and nobody has ten children to start a whole new school! Hale would die a slow death, the final nail in the coffin being when the last of the young people leave to make their family somewhere else."

"That's right," added Eve. "Leaving us old folks to die out here one by one until there's nothing left but more old houses and overgrown fields."

"My word, that is a depressing image," said Flo.

"Not depressing," replied Min. "Now we have a teacher."

I added, "Needing ten students to open a small school is quite a conundrum."

"Don't even know what that word means," said Eve. "Pretty soon my boys will have more words in their heads than me."

"*Conundrum* means a kind of contradiction, something that does not make sense."

"Well, closing a school and needing so many students to reopen it in a place like this, then, is a—how do you say it?—a con...undrum.' Is also stupid and mean."

"That too!"

"Can we talk about my Orris again?"

"Why Pearl, by all means."

"He's a true sweetie, that one is." Min smiled.

Pearl clapped her hands, pinkness flowing into her cheeks, her blue eyes sparkling. Thin, ghostly light hair tied in a ponytail framed Pearl's narrow heart-shaped face. Except for faint lines around her eyes, she looked twelve, particularly if you went by her figure.

"Orris, he is wonderful. I mean, nothing special, can't say nothing like that. Just special. To me."

Flo tapped Pearl on her knee. "Naturally, your boy is special, to all of us."

"Absolutely," I said as Eve and Min nodded.

"But I am not, so he is not."

"You are both special."

Pearl became quiet.

"Tell me what Orris likes to do," I prodded.

"Well, he likes to eat. To sleep. And he likes looking at the stars."

"Looking at the stars?"

"Yes. His bedroom is that one."

Pearl pointed to the southwest corner of their house gracing the opposite side of the harbor. Her home did not look so decrepit on such a clear, pretty day.

"When I check on him at night, he's often sitting on the floor looking outside, staring at the stars. Sometimes I cover the window with a sheet to make him go to sleep."

"The boy is curious, that is good."

"Anyway, that's all what he likes. We don't talk about stars around Leroy. Leroy don't see no point knowing about anything but fishing." Pearl glanced at the harbor and then back at us.

"Well, we can teach so that everyone is happy. Orris can fish *and* learn, for life is big enough for both."

"I sure like that!"

"Pearl, might you also send Jon to school?"

Eve rolled her eyes.

Pearl chuckled, confirming what I expected.

"Why, Leroy wouldn't never approve of that."

"Well, you see, actually, it is the law that he goes."

Pearl turned even more pale. "The law?"

Eve clicked her tongue. "That's ridiculous! Pearl's not breaking the law. Jon's sixteen."

"Maine was one of the earliest states to pass its compulsory school attendance law. In 1875. Ages seven to seventeen."

"What does *compulsory* mean?" asked Eve.

"Means must do," answered Flo.

"That's hogwash! There's no way my Irv and Sam will stay in school past sixteen, neither!"

"I am afraid Eve is right," added Min. "American law don't apply much to Popplestone Isle. Besides, the Hale school only goes to the eighth grade."

I turned to Min. "Technically, the law does apply, and Jon is supposed to travel uptown for high school, but from a practical perspective, I know he cannot. It is the same on Crescent for most boys."

Eve fixed her eyes firmly upon me. "Sixteen years in a place like Hale is high time for a young man to work."

"Sadly, is the way it is." Flo put her arm around Pearl, who still look scared.

"I understand," I surrendered. "I am sorry to alarm."

"So now, Pearl, when are you going to have another?" demanded Eve, changing the subject abruptly.

"I don't think—"

"Why not?"

"Well, there's Leroy, I mean, he's not..."

"Not what?"

"For goodness sake, let's all leave Pearl alone!" Flo's eyes flashed as she spoke.

"Then *you* have another," Eve snapped.

Flo frowned and placed one hand on her belly. "You know I can't."

"One girl around here isn't enough for a proper future."

I could stand it no longer and almost shouted, "Lucy is certainly enough!"

Flora continued, "We think so, too, thank you, Mildred. We are not sorry for only one. We are very blessed. Oh Min, oh dear, I did not mean—"

Min's eyes welled up. Not a sound came out of her pained face. Flo wrung her hands, then put one hand gently on Min's shoulder. Min flinched.

"Min, I...I did not mean how that sounded, please believe me."

Eve snorted.

"Be quiet, Eve!" I commanded. She glared at me.

"Min is as valuable as any mother here," I continued, looking at everyone sternly. "Why, on Crescent, it is women without their own flesh-and-blood children who are the best and most important aunties."

"Min often gives Orris snacks," offered Pearl.

"And my dear Lucy loves dropping by Min's house. Why, she is learning to sew, thanks to Min."

"Irv and Sam like your snacks, too," Eve added, concentrating on stirring her coffee again. "We...we do thank you for that."

"You see? Takes a whole town—or harbor—to raise a child."

Min took Flora's hand. "I so enjoy teaching Lucy to sew."

"Well, we are all harbor mothers here then, with a mighty good ratio of five women to four youngsters," I confirmed.

"You have one, we are five to five!" Pearl shouted.

Eve poked me in the stomach. "The sooner the better, Mildred."

I swatted her hand. "What if I cannot?"

"You must."

"My word!"

"I know, it's that bad," agreed Min. "You don't want to go through what I have, Mildred May, so get cracking. You're young. Thaddeus is strong. Shouldn't be a problem."

"Now it's time to leave Mildred alone," ordered Flo.

My face flushed. "I was hoping for a little bit of time."

"Everyone's watching," said Eve.

"And waiting," added Pearl.

"Not fair," said Min.

"Min's right," added Flo.

"Oh dear!" exclaimed Eve.

Little Sam dashed around the corner then and up the stairs. Without a glance at anyone but his ma, he jumped into Eve's lap, face streaming with tears.

The boy wrapped around her like a starfish clamping onto a mussel.

Eve held him tight. "I need to go."

"Certainly. Thank you for coming. If there is anything I can do—"

"Is fine."

The curtness in Eve's voice stopped me from pressing further.

As she walked away, Min said, "That boy cries easy."

Flo shook her head. "We don't know what happened. Who are we to judge?"

"Is just that most boys stop crying by his age."

"True, Min," I joined in. "But boys should be able to cry any time they want, their whole life. Would make for a whole lot healthier group of men."

"Maybe so."

"A man crying is better than him yelling." We all looked at Pearl, surprised by how forceful her voice had just become.

16

That evening we sat in our usual spot. The harbor was flat, and a deep navy-blue. Beyond the outer harbor to the horizon, the sea turned into such a creamy pale blue, she was almost white.

I set two slices of pecan pie on elegant red-and-white dessert plates. The fine china was from England, a wedding gift from the Perrys, a wealthy Crescent couple without children of their own who had taken interest in me since I was little.

"Thaddeus?"

"Yes?"

"I love you."

He grunted. Since that first morning together months before, he had not uttered those three precious words. I had been waiting.

"A grunt is all you can give me?"

"What do you want me to say?"

"That you love me back."

"You already know that."

"I like to hear it."

"Don't like to say it."

"I see."

"There's more important things to discuss, Mildred May. Winter's coming, for one."

"Why, it is only summer."

"Summer means fall. Fall means winter. Comes fast and bites you in the—"

"Thaddeus!"

"Arse."

"Where do we get wood?"

"Up on my hill there."

He pointed out the window to the western side of the harbor. Spruce trees packed a steep embankment rising near straight up into a mammoth boulder out by the entrance of the harbor. Many acres of evergreens surrounded the rock, stretching to the edge of the sea and farther inland, a striking contrast to the open fields.

"You ever go up to the very top of that rock?"

"Sometimes. Not often. Quite a view from up there. The whole harbor and everyone in it."

"Must be quite a sight."

"Nothing there to help come winter, though. Just a big old ledge. We clear below it, dragging the logs down the hill with oxen."

"I see. Will you need my help?"

"Need you to stack the wood after we do the lugging and sawing."

"We?"

"Irville, Marv, usually Todd and Rufus, and sometimes even that leech Leroy. My land. Miles's oxen. Miles and me, well, we get larger shares of the wood for the land and animal contributions."

"You mean Flora's and Miles's oxen."

Another grunt.

"My land."

"I will be there for you."

"I should say so, unless you be pregnant and can't lift much. Know that much."

I blushed at the thought, even sitting before my husband.

He continued, "You could be with child by now."

"That would be a little bit fast."

"Faster the better, Mildred. You're not getting any younger, got to hurry this along."

I wondered if he was in cahoots with the women, talking to me like that the very same day they had.

"How many do you want?"

"Ten."

"Ten?"

"Aim for ten. Maybe we'll get five. A few might die at birth, got to plan for that and be pregnant more."

"You rowed all the way to Crescent five times to woo me, and not a word about wanting ten children."

"Didn't want to scare you off. Was hard enough as it was to get you to say yes. Am telling you now."

I looked out to sea, imagining Crescent twelve miles due west after rounding the harbor corner. I suddenly wanted to be a little girl again, one of six children of my parents, in their house.

He looked at me with a wide grin. "As many as we can, at the least."

"I see. Are we negotiating?"

"Is for the good of the harbor, Mildred May. This here place means more to me than anything, I tell you."

"What about what is good for us? Ten children would spread us mighty thin. What do *you* want?"

"I want what's good for the harbor. Many babies be good for the harbor."

"Where will they sleep?"

"Will build bunk beds."

"And eat?"

"We have enough. Lobsters selling for eleven cents apiece now, should go up to twelve or thirteen cents next year, and I'm catching plenty. Said yourself we can live off the land here. And we can buy foodstuff from the Bells and from what's delivered by ship once a month from Robin Isle. You should plant a garden—should have this year. If you'd get out onto the beach more for clams and mussels and snails, well, there be plenty for free and we can save up faster for more children."

"I will forage more and plant a garden next year. But we start with one."

Another grunt. "'Course, how else do you start?! One baby, yes that'd be fine to start. Been waiting a long time to be a father."

"You have waited. And you deserve to be a father. I agree to one."

"Not negotiating!"

"Because you love me and want a family with me?"

"Because I love this here harbor of mine."

"And me?"

"And you. Together we will save Hale Harbor."

"I thought I married you, not the harbor."

"Jesus H. Christ, Mildred May!" Thaddeus gestured wildly, knocking his hand on the window by accident with a *thwunk*. "You marry me, you marry the harbor, simple as that. This is a good place. What are we arguing about?"

"Not arguing. Wondering."

"Wondering?"

"My role. Need to be loved. Told you that before."

"You're needed."

"Needed is different than loved."

"Same to me. Would it help if I said the words?"

"You have to mean them, Thaddeus."

"Love you," he said obediently.

"Mean that?"

"Yes, ma'am."

"Well, anyway, I love you."

"Aren't we going to eat supper soon? Need supper."

"Yes, that too."

I got up, kissed him on the forehead and went to the stove. Fish chowder and my Crescent Island famous popovers should do. I wondered how big a pot we would need as our family grew. Truth be told, I liked the idea of ten.

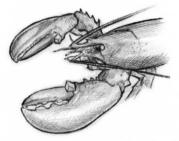

17

Wooden pegs keep a lobster's pincer and crusher claws closed.

A few days later and the fishing was fine.

"I've a mighty haul for you, my Mildred May!"

Thaddeus dropped a metal bucket of lobsters on the kitchen floor with a *clank*.

"Have at it, woman."

"My name is Mildred May."

"Have at it, Mildred May."

"That is better."

"No difference."

"There is to me. I will boil the water for our bugs. We are going to have a wondrous lobster stew this evening."

"Figured such. You're a good cook, I appreciate that."

"Why thank you, Thaddeus."

I picked up the buckets, glad for the wooden pegs jammed into the joints of pincer and crusher claws so they could not snap at me. The lobsters hissed and foamed from their tiny mouths, and their legs scraped the sides of the bucket sounding like fingernails on a chalkboard.

I stoked the fire. I always boiled up the water and then put lobsters in head-first, as they seemed to go fast that way. Never could stand watching those dark-green creatures trying to crawl out of a slowly heating-up pot.

The four cooked up bright red in fifteen minutes. I used my sewing scissors to slice down the middle of the tails and a rock to crush the claws. Was some grateful for fresh milk and butter from the incoming schooner that day, and for my herbs growing on the kitchen windowsill.

We sat as we always did at every meal. A blue-and-white check-ered tablecloth I'd brought from home draped the tiny table.

"The sea is turning angry, Thaddeus."

"That she is. Might not be fishing tomorrow, from the looks of her."

Darkened waves rolled in, churned up by wind that had been building all afternoon. That sea crashed on the rocks below the house.

"The water is so gray, same as the sky today."

"Pulling up the mudflats as they come in, them waves are. Clams must be sucking themselves down deep."

"Indeed."

"Full moon tonight. Expect a very high tide."

"Thaddeus?"

"Yes?"

"In a storm, if it happens with a full moon, well, does the water ever come up, you know, too far?"

"You are asking about storms again."

"Yes."

"You are asking if water reaches the house?"

I did not like his question. I could not bear the thought.

"Yes."

"Never."

"That is a relief."

"There's plenty of spray, mind you, if a southerly be whipping tips off the waves and blowing them into the house. Salts up windows. Paid Pearl to clean them before. Now I've got you."

"A southerly storm sounds a little rough."

"Remember what I told you about using the clothesline to go out to the shitter...ah, outhouse."

"I will."

"Harbor's for everyone, Mildred May. She provides. But she can be a mean old bitch, too, gets mighty harsh around here in a squall."

"Thaddeus, please, the language!"

"Sorry."

"Are storms why there are so many abandoned houses around?"

"Nope. Them families just up and left."

"Must have been empty for some time, given the ramshackle shape they are in now."

"Going to use them houses for firewood one of these days."

"What happened?"

"Damn shame! Had eight children in the schoolhouse back then, with Lucy and Orris babies at home. Two barren couples and two couples with children left the harbor together. Them childless couples had to go, wanted them gone. Other two families, damn traitors, left too. One of the fathers was the teacher."

"I do not understand."

"Weren't making babies. Had to go."

"My word, how unfair! What about Marv and Min?"

"Marv's family. Wish they'd make one, though. Min's not doing what she should."

"Thaddeus! Takes two to make a child. Surely they have tried."

"Not hard enough."

"Those families, they had homes. Land. And work. Besides the teacher, what did they do?"

"The other three men and the two wives with no babies fished. The mothers stayed at home. I made it tough as nails on the water for the...um...for the childless couples, and they gave up trying. Problem was, they took two good families with them. Didn't figure on those four parents going, too! Was the one mistake I ever made in my life. Six school children and the teacher, gone in a day. I sure messed up good. We've got to make up for that now."

"We?"

"We."

"You scared them off."

"Yes, I scared them off."

"And now I have to birth out ten babies to make up for it?"

"You sure are smart."

I actually grunted.

"Good chowder, Mildred. Nine would be okay. As long as you keep teaching, too."

I sighed, "I do like my chowder, going to have another helping. Give me your bowl, Thaddeus, it needs filling, too."

18

"Never met a man secure in himself, not a dang one, makes them moody," Min said, sipping coffee. We sat on my porch. She had come by and started in without asking if I had time. So much to do that day, but Min was family. Truth be told, I welcomed the interruption.

"Really?"

"And when the men can't talk with each other worth the salt for a single sardine, it's us women getting everyone back on track."

"Popplestone is a lot like Crescent that way."

"Island women hold up most of the sky. Just like how you stuck up for me the other day, saying I was everyone's auntie. I like that. Came by to thank you."

Min, you are a fine woman, and I sure am glad you are my sister-in-law."

"I am glad to finally have a sister-in-law, and one so not like the others."

"'Not like the others' is what Lucy said to me my first day here! What does it mean?"

"You don't know?"

"No."

"All the women Thaddeus tried out."

"Tried out?"

"He was looking for a wife."

"Well, a single fellow has the right to court."

"Worked them sixteen hours a day—funny way to court a gal."

"They stayed with Thaddeus?"

"Good gracious no, they all lived with me and Miles. Thing is, before his house was built, Thaddeus stayed with us, too. People assumed things. I assure you nothing happened between them except maybe a kiss or two."

"How many?"

"How many kisses?"

"How many women."

"Five or six."

"Why didn't any of them work out?"

"Well, don't rightly know. One gal cried and cried. She was tiny, smaller than Pearl, not strong enough for this life. Another never said a word, strange one she was. I can't remember the others so well, been a couple years now since the last one. One seemed to have possibility, but she left suddenly in a huff, mad as hell at Thaddeus about something. He had them digging for clams, painting the house, cooking up special meals. I tried to help them, but Thaddeus made each woman cook on her own, even for Miles and me. Made them pick crabmeat until their hands got raw, clean the shed, barn, and house top to bottom, even painting his buoys, *and* even cleaning the outhouse! Worked them to the bone, he did."

"No wonder they left."

"Plus, none of them were teachers."

"I heard about the teacher leaving with his family. That was a terrible blow to Hale, I gather."

"Well, now we've got a teacher again, thanks to you and Thaddeus."

"I would hope Thaddeus married me for me, not because of what I do."

"Mildred May, this be a hurting place. Whoever lands here needs to...well...be a good fit and stay. Thaddeus chose a big strong teacher, nothing wrong with that."

"Yes, I see, when you put it that way. Just had no idea about those women. Where did they go?"

"Some of them live in uptown Popplestone now. Others in America. Thing is, once he sent one packing, people assumed, you know, um, that she was experienced after that and not so marriageable."

"You mean my husband ruined women without even sleeping with them?"

"You sure are blunt!"

"Guess I am. Too much so, is what some people say."

"Don't worry about those women, who they are or anything like that. You're different from them. Stronger. You'll do fine here. We want you to do fine. We are even glad you're from away. Need new blood and want you to stay. You are teaching our children!"

Min calling me "from away" reminded me of Todd and I chatting about the same thing and me feeling welcomed then. How Min described me from away made me feel trapped.

"Where has Todd been?" I blurted.

"Todd? Not my fella, don't keep track of him."

"Thought you kept track of everybody."

"You calling me a gossip?"

"No!"

"Well then, I did hear from Eve she saw Todd biking up to town and that he hasn't been back for a week or so. Probably some job up there. Lord knows there's not enough work in Hale for a carpenter-woodworker."

"I see."

"Why do you care?"

"I do not care."

"Seems like you care."

"Do you think Thaddeus would have still rowed all the way to Crescent if I was not a teacher?"

Min eyed me closely. "Honestly, probably not."

"I see." I looked deep into my coffee.

Min put her hand on my forearm. "Mildred May, Thaddeus *loves* you, too, everyone can see that."

"I...I hope so. I think so."

"Do you love him?"

"Yes."

"Well then, you are both on your way, then."

"On our way?"

"To marital bliss."

"Marital bliss—now that sounds nice."

"It is, and I am always right about affairs of the heart."

"You sound like a poet."

"Nope, no poet. I just say the damn straight truth."

"Okay, Min, I will trust you are right about affairs of the heart, including for Thaddeus and me."

"Good. I think I will have myself a third donut. All this serious talk makes me hungry."

Min turned a chocolate one over, seemingly pleased to see coconut flakes covering the bottom side, too.

"The recipe is free."

"Wouldn't dare. Teacher Gale's donuts are going to be the talk of the island. Don't need to compete with that, neither."

19

"What you been up to all dang day?"

Thaddeus had just walked in from fishing after my afternoon with Min.

"I do not like your tone, Thaddeus."

"Don't like the laundry not being done, Mildred."

"The chickens are fed."

"The counters are dirty."

"The windows are washed."

"There's clutter on the table."

"The floors are swept. Bedroom walls and steps are scrubbed. More of your socks are darned. Your bath is ready in the barn so you do not need to go up to the pond. And supper is ready when you are done your bath. Not enough?"

"We're not summer rusticators, having time to laze around."

"I do not laze around!"

"Saw you on the porch gossiping."

"Min dropped by. She is your sister-in-law. We are not slaves."

"Not slaves, you be right there—wrong color."

"Thaddeus, my word! Where did that come from? That is not nice to say at all."

"Around here, ever see a nig—?"

"Stop it! Negroes are not slaves and have as much right as anyone to live here. You have never even seen a slave. Maine was admitted to the Union as a free state eighty-eight years ago. Slavery ended forty-seven years ago, ten years before you were born! My grandfather fought in the Civil War, you know, lost a leg. His commanding officer was Joshua Chamberlain. You insult my grandfather. You insult Joshua Chamberlain."

He grunted.

"Not having this conversation until you are more respectful." I stomped my feet.

"Fine."

We sat down, uncomfortably silent for a while. I burned inside, hating how the man had just spoken of others and disrespected hard-won history.

After some time he bragged, "I've seen a few colored folks in my day, you know.

"Do not care."

"Thought you cared about colored folk."

"I do care. I just do not care if you saw one, is all. What a silly thing to say. What you have seen or have not seen is meaningless. People are people, however they look."

"Okay then, won't talk about it. What's important is what we be eating tonight."

"My ma's fish casserole. You will like it."

"I'd better."

"Go take your bath. You smell of rotten fish."

"Smell of money, my dear, you know that."

"I still do not like the stench."

"Will take a bath, then. And think of you while having it."

"Get out of here. The conversation today has been most unpleasant."

"People is people, you just said. You have who I am. I am the greatest around here. Should be more than enough for you. You live nicer than you did on Crescent."

I snorted.

Thaddeus came back into the kitchen from his bath, put his hand on my shoulder, startling me into a jump. "I am sorry, Mildred May, I truly am."

"My goodness, is that a tear in your eye?"

"No tear."

"What are you sorry for?"

"My mean words. About colored folk. People are people, you be right there, don't matter the color. And...and what your grandfather did for America, well, he is a hero. Along with Chamberlain."

"It takes a lot for someone to apologize and really mean it. Thank you, Thaddeus. If I may, I believe *Negro* is better to say than *colored*."

"Negro. I will remember."

"Good."

Hands in his pockets, Thaddeus looked at his feet and said, "Thank you for making me a better man."

I took his hands in mine, and then kissed him on both cheeks.

"I like being your wife. That is, for the most part, when you are nice."

"I will try harder."

We quietly ate supper looking out over our harbor from our little table with the pretty checkered tablecloth.

"Never tire of these mussels." Thaddeus threw a couple of blue shells into an empty bowl with a clatter. "Try adding a bit of whiskey next time. Mighty good with a bit of whiskey."

"I will do that. Thaddeus?"

"Yes, Mildred."

"What if I—we, I mean—cannot have a child?"

"What?"

"It has only been a few months of trying, nothing to be worried about. And yet, one never knows about these things."

Thaddeus threw an uneaten mussel back onto his plate. "We have to."

"I am just saying, what if."

"Don't like the what if!"

"Me neither. I am just saying."

He picked the mussel back up and noisily sucked out the meat.

"Don't worry so much. Hear worrying about it makes it hard to get one. Don't understand that, but maybe is true. So just stop worrying."

"What is wrong with having another plan, just in case?"

"Another plan? What would that be? Stealing a baby from somewhere? You either have one, or more, or you don't. Mildred May, why are you so set on complicating everything?"

"I like to plan."

"Me too, about fishing or money. Not ever at supper. Tired."

"I'll grant you that."

"What?"

"Means I give you that—that is, I understand what you just said."

"I see."

"Maybe we should have an English lesson now."

"Seems we just did."

"Just so."

"What else can you teach me?"

"Well, let's see. Have you ever heard of a pun?"

"Pun? No. You sure know a lot of words. And United States history."

"Pun. Something that means two things at the same time because of the context. Context is how a word is used in a sentence. So, a pun can have two meanings at once, or even three, depending on the context."

"Give me an example. I like this talk better than fighting."

"Okay, let me think for a moment."

Thaddeus sucked the meat out of a tiny periwinkle shell with a loud, *schlooooop* while he waited. Supper smelled of the salty sea. Everything on our plates except for the melted butter had come from the beach.

"Okay, how is this: 'Flora has to go to America to pick up some medicine. She is traveling for Miles.'"

"Miles is sick?"

"No, not really, but yes he is in this example. This is a pun, see.

She is traveling for—to help—Miles. She is also traveling many miles."

"I get it! I like puns!"

"I'm glad."

"Sunday is coming up. Time for my reading lessons."

"That is right."

"Another pun."

"How so?"

"You said, 'That is right.' Like, I am right, so you agreed. Is also 'right'—a good thing—to do."

"Thaddeus, yes, exactly so! You identified a pun. Very good."

"I ain't so stupid after all."

"Never heard anyone call you stupid. You are not stupid."

"That's right."

I leaned to him, brushed his cheek, and said, "Seems I am starting to love you to the stars and back."

20

Quahog clam (left) and mya arenaria "steamer" clam

"Pearl!" I called out as she walked briskly across the beach some days later.

The tiny woman looked up. She held a small basket of whelks, those larger cousins of thumbnail-size periwinkles.

"Please do me a favor and take some donuts home."

Pearl ran to the edge of our property, where I met her with a basket of a dozen donuts.

She eyed them closely. "Oh, but I couldn't."

"I made too many. They will end up as chicken feed if you do not help me out," I fibbed.

Pearl looked at the donuts again, perhaps imagining my hens pecking them to dust.

"Thank you. My menfolk will be some happy about these."

"Make sure you eat some, too, Pearl. *Pearl.* My oh my, you have a good name for a fisherman's wife. Especially here in Hale Harbor, so full of steamers and those big quahogs. Perhaps you will find a Hale Harbor pearl someday."

Pearl looked startled again, as if that were the first time anyone had ever paid her such a compliment. Which was exactly why I had said it.

"Would be nice," she replied.

Pearl walked along our yard, delicately stepping down the stone steps to the beach, trotting home along sunbaked seaweed—the turning tide line. The dead seaweed crunched under her feet. She clutched the handle of that basket as if it held bars of silver.

"That was mighty nice to do for Pearl and her family."

"Todd. I did not see you from behind the barn. You beach foraging, too?"

"Yes, clams for supper tonight."

"The sea provides."

"She certainly does."

"I am sorry I have no more donuts to give to you this day."

"Pearl needs them more. I do, however, look forward to trying them one day. Mildred's donuts are the talk of the harbor."

"Really?"

"Really."

"Todd?"

"Yes?"

"You have time for a longer chat?"

"With you, certainly."

We sat on a couple of boulders on the edge of the shore and started on about the island and the sea, the wild plants one could pick and eat, and the abundance of seafood in Hale Harbor. Soon I found myself telling Todd that Thaddeus wanted ten children. I had to share that with someone, and did not dare mention it to Min, who had none, or to any of the others, who would chatter about it.

Todd laughed before he replied. "More children than adults in Hale would make for a blessed handful for us all, especially for you."

"Indeed they would. The more the merrier!"

"You will be the most wonderful mother."

"Why thank you, Todd! But why do you say so?"

"Just a feeling I get. Can tell."

"I like your feelings about me as a mother."

"Me too."

An hour later, he tipped his brown cap and continued along the beach.

By then, I could see Leroy and Jon Jennings making way to shore from their day at sea, Jon rowing, Leroy in the stern.

Jon employed sharp, disjointed strokes to his rowing. The boat leaped forward and then stalled until the next pull, not making way very well.

Leroy glared at his son.

Thaddeus, Irville, and Marvin headed to shore on our side in two boats. They made way smooth as silk, but with expressions grim and gruff.

21

"Been chatting all day again?"

I set my pot of boiled potatoes on the kitchen counter and let out a sigh.

"Thaddeus, I had donuts with Pearl. A few minutes of talk! The rest of the time, I worked as usual."

"And that Calderwood bloke?"

"Same. Todd was walking by. He said hello on his way."

"You call him Todd?"

"Why yes, nobody is formal around here."

"Was a long hello. What did you talk about?"

"The clams he dug for his supper. How he planned to cook them," I answered dutifully. Did not lie. Just did not tell him all. It was none of his business we had talked about babies and mothering.

"He's got to stay away from our beach. Them clams be ours."

"Thaddeus, my word, there are too many. Everyone in the harbor could eat steamers every night, and there'd still be more for the next year growing faster than we could all eat them."

"Our house. Our beach."

"The beach is everyone's."

"More ours than anyone's."

"I do not see it that way."

"The rest of the world works the full day, Mildred, not a lot of chatting."

"I learned about Orris from Pearl," I fibbed again. Thaddeus could not know I had been charitable with food at his expense. "Students are my job, for school."

"You're not getting paid for today."

"Talking with my students' mothers is like...is like, well, like you preparing gear for fishing."

A grunt.

"I mean it, Thaddeus. A small amount of time is all, to make me a better teacher. For our harbor children. Your precious harbor's children! This place means everything to you, said so yourself. You want Hale's children to get good educations, am I correct?"

"Just get all your jobs done in the house. Including a decent lunch for me. I get the worst packed lunches of the bunch, and I'm the boss of them boys. Is downright embarrassing."

"I will put more in your lunch. But Thaddeus, you may be the boss of them, but you are not the boss of me."

"Yes I am."

"A husband is not his wife's boss, he is her partner."

"In my house, the husband is the boss. That be me."

"Not how it works on Crescent."

"We are on Popplestone."

"Far as I can tell, not how it works on Popplestone, either."

"This is really Gale Harbor, you know, only says Hale Harbor on them charts!"

"My word, what has gotten into you? A bad day on the sea does not mean harping on your wife at home."

"Just get on with supper. And it better be good."

I stood there, arms crossed.

"Please," he finally added.

I turned on my heel and fumed into the kitchen.

Thaddeus took his bath.

22

As fall settled in and afternoons got chillier, the occasional maples amongst the island's spruce turned to vivid orange and yellow. V-shaped flocks of geese regularly flew over our house heading south. My cherished great blue heron pair would soon take their journey to warmer places, as well. Ground animals began to disappear, and the incessant deer flies and mosquitoes mercifully evaporated. The harbor became quieter, subdued.

We never talked about who was boss again. We made love nearly every night, though given how tired I was most of the time, I would have preferred far less. No regular Sunday reading lessons for Thaddeus. Some chore or another nearly always got in our way. I hated how lovemaking had become one of the chores.

On September 22nd, the evening before my first day at Hale Harbor school, I pulled my navy-blue apron around my stomach, pleased with how much string was left to tie the bow. Felt like I ate a pile at every meal, even more than usual. Yet there I was, a smaller waist, still ample hips, and more buxom than ever. I started to enjoy how I looked for the first time.

"Hello, Mildred," Thaddeus said softly, walking in from his day at sea.

"*Yech!* Thaddeus, go wash yourself! You smell worse than a skunk! My eyes are stinging."

"Smell of money, my dear girl. Smell of money."

Thaddeus said that often and watched every penny I spent. I had not even dared send my letter to Ma, lest he complain about the postage.

"Your tub is waiting for you in the barn."

"I'm going."

Almost six o'clock and he returned, smelling mighty fragrant, in a nice way. I ladled thick, milky broth into Thaddeus's bowl, covering the delicate design of my treasured china.

Thaddeus drank directly from his bowl, slurping loudly, steam floating in front of his face like a thin veil.

"Thaddeus?"

"Yes?"

"How about a little party here this weekend with everyone in the harbor, to celebrate the first week of school?"

"Party? Everyone? Even them Jennings dogs?"

"Yes, even the Jennings *men*. We cannot invite some and not the others with only seventeen in Hale. Five couples, four children and Jon, the two single fellows—why, it would be so fine! Young Jon Jennings, well I know he is not *all* right, he should not have poached your pots, but if he sees how we treat folks, he will do better. The boy has plenty of growing and learning ahead."

"His father, Leroy, is the nasty one, probably too much of a coward to steal himself. Puts his own son up to it. Damn son of a bitch. And after I let them have a cut of the herring, too. He just don't know when to quit."

"Do you have to curse so much?"

"I do. Not changing. You'll have to get used to it."

"I will never get used to it. But I will not nag you about it, neither."

Thaddeus raised one eyebrow. "I guess I can agree to that."

"Supper Saturday then, here. Everyone."

"Got to be music. Tell Eve to have Irville bring his mandolin. Marvin needs his accordion. Flo, her fiddle. That's all I have to say about it. I'll be here, not smelling of bait, fresh flannel shirt if you have one for me. Whatever makes you happy."

I got up, faced him, took off his cap, and gently placed my right hand behind his head. I silently took his bowl away with my other hand as I kissed him.

I then slowly lifted my green-and-white-striped skirt above my knees, watching Thaddeus's eyes glaze over as I did.

I liked being the starter, for once.

"Yes," he whispered.

I sat facing him, my ample legs on either side of his muscled ones, swelling breasts barely touching his broad chest through our clothes. I kissed him long and slow, the only time he would be quiet that night.

23

We were up at five a.m. the following day.

"My lessons! I will be fired my first day!"

"Won't be fired. Nobody else to teach."

"But I want to do well."

"You will. That director of unorganized territories can't deny you the right to make more babes for his school, now can he?"

"Oh, you think I should tell him why I'm not prepared my first day?"

"Maybe you should."

"Maybe I will. Or maybe you will take eggs on toast this morning right quick instead of that slow oatmeal you like, so I can get to work on those lessons."

"Eggs be fine."

I blew him a kiss, and he mimicked it hitting his cheek just like my little brother Foster used to.

I ran out the door to the small shed behind the house. Henrietta and Harriet pecked at my hand and screeched when I reached for their eggs.

I slapped them between the eyes. "Shush!"

Four eggs for Thaddeus. Three for me. A perfect start to the week.

24

A short walk past Brownes' and I arrived at work early my first day. The unpainted schoolhouse featured two tall windows and a simple entry staircase built on top of a large, moss-covered boulder. I had spent a good week cleaning the insides top to bottom with help from the ladies. Todd had repaired the legs of two desks, reattached the screen door drifting off its hinges, and replaced four clapboards on the shaded side where water damage had eaten parts of the wood. He took four of the ten desks outside to sand and apply several thin layers of varnish to them. Most importantly, he had cleaned the creosote out of the potbelly's stovepipe, protecting the building and us from a chimney fire.

"Next summer, we should paint the schoolhouse," he had announced after inspecting clapboards and window trim on each side of the building. "I'll see to it."

Within the hour, my students arrived, led by the youngest. Lucy opened the door, her mouth twitching into little smiles, her brown and blue eye sparkling. She wore a billowy white shirt and a long denim skirt with fringes of white lace just above her ankles.

"May we come in now?"

"Yes, welcome!"

Irville, the oldest at ten, sauntered in with a serious expression on his face, hands in the pockets of brown trousers so short, could see bare leg above his long black socks.

"Where do we sit?"

"Youngest in front, older ones in back," I suddenly decided.

Orris, his sandy hair flopping about, ran past Irville and sat next to Lucy in his metal chair attached to the pine desk.

Orris's eyes darted away from me—to the chalkboard, window, and door. Surely, he wanted to escape! He tapped his feet together. The boy wore mismatched socks poking through shoes with the fronts cut off.

Samuel slid into his seat behind Orris and fidgeted just as much.

Samuel placed his and Irville's lunch basket on the floor between their desks. Sam looked four years younger than his one-year-older brother Irville. Sam's feet did not even touch the floor, and he swam in his deep-red long-sleeved shirt and brown trousers, cinched tight around the waist with an old rope. Eve must have had Irv wear clothes just as long as he could squeeze into them before passing them on to his brother, for whom they would still be too big.

Sam's thick, wavy blond hair was a contrast to his brother's fine, short black hair. Samuel's face was angular while Irville's round. I could not help but remember what Thaddeus had told me about young Sam: "That boy looks nothing like Irville Senior. Guess that Smith fella wasn't run off the island fast enough."

Boys and girl sat with their hands in their laps, eyes wide, the silence thick with anticipation. The room was bare, save a black chalkboard and bright bouquet of goldenrod in a glass jar.

"I forgot your apple!" Lucy rummaged through her bag until she pulled one out, triumphantly putting it on my desk.

"We have one for you, too," said Irville.

"I didn't bring one, sorry," added Orris.

"Two apples are more than enough for this teacher."

I faced my charges, each one sitting straight up and attentive, the boys wide-eyed. I grinned. "I am not going to bite you."

Lucy covered her mouth with her hand as she giggled. The boys looked sideways at each other, two of them sporting awkward smiles.

"I will not hit you, either, not ever." I looked straight at a frowning Orris.

"I do not believe in that, the hitting. I do believe in good behavior, though. You will all behave well, won't you?"

"Yes, ma'am!" they chorused.

"Good! Now children, I have three rules we must all live by, including me. Number one, you come to school with clean nails."

Lucy laughed as the boys inspected their fingers, discovered how blackened their nails were, and collectively grimaced. Orris sat on his hands.

"Starting tomorrow is soon enough."

The brothers put down their hands. Orris pulled his out from under him.

"Number two, finish your lessons on time.

And number three, never be late for school. That is, without a good excuse explained by your parents."

The seven-, eight-, nine-, and ten-year-olds nodded vigorously, Lucy's and Samuel's abundant golden hair flying about.

"Well, all right then! This is some fine and dandy start to a year of education. I am in gratitude of your attitudes."

There was high-pitched laughter in return, and another Lucy-giggle.

I handed Maine state-issued writing workbooks to six eager hands, but Orris Jennings kept his in his lap. The lad stared at his desk.

The boy had to know that what happened in boats had no connection to my classroom. The school was *my* territory, plain and simple. I gently placed his book on his desk and said, "I am glad you are my student."

Orris looked up and nodded.

"Much better," I encouraged Irville on his writing.

"Why do we need to write like this? Am going to be a fisherman."

"Fishermen need to write."

"Why?"

"You might need to send a letter to the Governor of Maine someday."

Irv and Sam laughed.

"Indeed you may. If not the governor, perhaps somebody in town. The world is more complicated than in the old days and will be getting even more complex. Like, maybe someone's bull gets loose and does damage to your home. You would need to document what happened in order to receive compensation from the bull's owner."

"What?"

"Please say 'pardon,' it is more polite."

"Pardon?"

"You will need to write about the problem so the owner of the bull can pay you money for what the bull wrecked."

"Oh."

Lucy jumped out of her seat. "So learning to write helps with money, isn't that so, Teacher Gale?"

"Exactly right, my dear."

"That's what Ma and Pa say. They did that once. Someone did something bad to them. My mother wrote some letters and got some money. That's how we bought the land here."

"Well then, that is an excellent example! Thank you, Lucy."

Irv scowled and gripped his pencil even harder, near the pointy end.

"Irville, relax. Loosen your fingers and set them back a bit on the pencil and the writing will become easier."

"Yes, ma'am."

"You are getting neater, I see that. Good work, young man."

"Yes, ma'am, thank you, ma'am."

And so it went for the morning: writing, reading, checking, and two play breaks outside. Students always perform better after running about.

Time flew by. Lucy was way ahead of the three older boys, annoying them to no end. To keep her quietly occupied, I gave her *Alice's Adventures in Wonderland*, one of dozens of good books owned by the school.

Orris rubbed his stomach. "When's lunch?"

His eyes had that deep hollow stare that happens when a child is hungry, reminding me of my often famished brothers about to erupt into some terrible ruckus.

"The sun is overhead. Seems now would be a good time for lunch, how about that?"

"Yes, ma'am!"

"Yes, ma'am!"

"Yes, ma'am!"

"Yes, ma'am!"

Lucy set her basket on her desk and with both hands lifted something wrapped in a thick red napkin. She peeked inside the cloth, licked her lips, and mouthed, *Thank you, Mommy.* More quickly then, she pulled out a large roll filled with ham, tomatoes, and cheese, a tiny wisp of steam curling from its top. A heated rock had kept her lunch warm all morning.

Orris held a big brown piece of bread packed with nuts and fruits, gobbling it quickly. A glass of tea rounded out his simple yet healthful meal.

Irville and Samuel pulled thick sandwiches out of their baskets, butter slathered between the meat and bread. Like their schoolmates, they ate with two hands, elbows on the desks, devouring those sandwiches in chomps.

I relished the quiet that followed as I ate a chunk of cheese, two donuts, and the apples, and vowed to set a better example with my next day's lunch.

The school day ended well before I was ready.

"I don't want to go home yet," whined Orris.

Lucy took Orris's hand. "Me either. But I'll dance you home, on my way to mine."

"Okay! You dance. I will skip."

"Okay!"

When the four children trotted out of hearing distance, Orris wearing his lunch basket on his head like a tiara, I bellowed, "These are *my* children too, now! We do not need any more in Hale Harbor. Why, this is already perfect!"

25

The second morning start of school, Lucy trudged up the steps. No dancing. She and the Thomas brothers quietly slipped into their seats and stayed silent.

"And where is our young Master Jennings today?"

Irv and Sam looked down so hard I was afraid they would bore actual holes through their freshly stained desks. Lucy looked up at me, her blue and brown eye uncharacteristically stormy.

"What is it, Lucy?"

"He's...he's in the shed!" Tears rolled down her cheeks.

"Why, whatever for?"

"Something, don't know what. He's crying now. Or was, when I went by. Tried to get him out. Darn door was latched up high! Couldn't reach!"

I winced, forgave Lucy's swear, tried to ignore the pit in my stomach, and picked up the chalk. Turning my back on the students, I started writing lessons, seething inside. This sort of thing had happened on Crescent.

I wrote the day's multisyllabic word *diligently* into sample sentences, the familiar feel and sound of chalk on blackboard calming me some.

"You should go get him!"

I turned around, chalk in midair. Lucy stood right behind me. "I beg your pardon?"

"Yeah, go get him!" Irville stood, fists clenched, arms back as if he was trying to fly.

"Please, Mrs. Gale!" Lucy's little face squirreled up so hard she actually produced wrinkles.

"I am not supposed to leave the schoolhouse. This is a state rule."

"We will behave. We promise! Right, boys?"

Agreed Irville, "Right! Won't go nowhere."

"Right-o!" Samuel stood up as tall as he could make himself.

I lowered my arm slowly and placed the chalk on my desk, pausing as I looked at those determined faces.

"Well, all right, then, I am off. When I come back, I want to see your alphabet handwriting practice sheets, as many as you can manage. Your best quality. And think about our new word for today, *diligently*."

"Yes, ma'am!"

"Yes, ma'am!"

"Yes, ma'am! We will be diligently!"

"*Diligently* describes a verb, Lucy. That's called an adverb."

"We will diligently study, then!"

"Very good!"

I draped my light-blue sweater over my shoulders, opened the screen door, and looked behind me. Irville, Samuel, and Lucy were bent over their desks, pencils held with purpose.

I left, determined to fulfill mine.

26

I walked toward the harbor on the main road, then headed east down a narrow way leading to every Hale Harbor house except for ours and the Brownes'. Grass climbed high along the path's center, even past my waist in some areas. Horses and buggies rarely came to Hale.

Four deer grazed for flowers among the weeds. A rabbit darted in front of me, rustling as it vanished into the grass. Eve hung laundry by her home on my left, the only house facing straight down the center of the harbor. Thankfully, her back was to me, ponytail bobbing as she whistled *Yankee Doodle*. I trotted past, holding one arm under my chest to ease a painful bounce.

I slowed at Rufus Mank's tiny place, a shack I had first thought was another abandoned house. Awkward piles of gnarled rope littered the way to the man's front door—a set of boards barely hanging on with one rusty hinge—along with broken traps, old shipping boxes, and broken glass bottles.

Then came the Calderwood home peeking through the spruce trees. As messy as Rufus's house was, Todd's was neat and pretty, with bright flower assortments in blue-painted window boxes against white clapboards.

"Mildred?"

The man occupying my thoughts stepped from behind a spruce.

"Good morning, Todd."

"Good morning to you. It is not a school day?"

"Well, I...yes, indeed it is. Orris did not make it this morning, and we are all a bit worried about him."

"I am sorry to hear that. Is there anything I can do to help?"

"No, no thank you."

"I would really like to help."

"No need. Um, well maybe there is."

"Anything Mildred. I would do anything for the children. And for you."

"I know. Why is that, Todd?"

"Well, I don't know. I guess because children are naturally special. And you, you are important to the children, so you are important to me."

"That simple?"

"And I like you being my friend. The menfolk here, you know, with the exception of Rufus, they are all married. Rufus is fine, I have no issue with him. Is just that—"

"You and Rufus are very different."

"That's right."

"He is messy, and you are neat."

"Yes, there is that."

"You must be lonely, being the only single, neat fellow in the harbor."

Todd laughed. "I guess that's it, yes."

"Well, I am very glad to be your friend. Although I must warn you, I am not nearly as neat as you are." I looked around him at his house.

"I am grateful. What is it, friend, not-perfectly-neat Mildred, that I can do to help with Orris? He is the man of the hour here, not me."

"Did you see Leroy and Jon go out to fish today? Things are not so right at the Jennings house. Orris may have been punished by his father. I would feel better dropping by if I knew Leroy was not home."

"Oh no, that's terrible! Outrageous! Rest assured, Leroy's out fishing with Jon, I am absolutely sure of it. He rather stomped off this morning."

"You are angry. Me, too. I appreciate your feelings."

"I'll keep an eye on little Orris and Pearl, even Jon. I live so close by. If anything doesn't look right, I will help them, that's a promise."

"Thank you, Todd."

"I'll be on my way, then. I'm looking for mushrooms. And you have a mission to accomplish. Wait, shall I come with you?"

"Best I manage on my own. If two of us show up, we might startle Pearl and Orris more than is necessary."

Todd tipped his light-brown cap. "Good luck finding our young academic, Mildred."

"He is a smart boy."

"He is."

I continued on, creating new sentences for the day's word. "I am *diligently* looking for my student. I hope my students are *diligently* studying in my absence. Todd is *diligently* looking for mushrooms."

I made it to the Jennings home in minutes, a plain Foursquare atop a knoll looking out to sea and across the harbor to Thaddeus's alongshore wharf made of granite blocks.

I was some grateful for Todd's assurance that only Pearl and Orris would be home. Thaddeus had warned me about Leroy Jennings before, saying, "He's no good, up to no good, just no good" and even, "He should leave Hale Harbor *for* good."

I looked at the windowless, slanted, unpainted shed next to the main house. I walked slowly, listening carefully. There was no crying as Lucy had heard earlier. I knocked on the house door. An alarmed, pale face at the window relaxed when Pearl recognized me. A lock undone. A lock? Way out here? She opened the door.

"What a surprise! I will put on some tea."

"My dear Pearl!"

"Is nothing."

"It is not nothing!"

"I am all right."

"You need to put some raw meat on that eye. Your face is swollen something terrible!"

"No meat here."

"Do you have anything else to put on it?"

"Don't have much."

"And Orris? We all miss him at school."

Pearl looked at her ragged slippers. "Orris isn't feeling too well today."

"May I see him?"

"Yes."

We walked into a living room bare of furniture save an old gray couch. The sofa leaked shreds of white stuffing, some of it drifting through cracks to the basement between unpainted floorboards. Orris slept, arms by his side, head resting on his left cheek.

"Leroy did that," I hissed, nodding to the dark-purple ring around his right eye.

"Can't do nothing to stop Leroy when he gets into the rum. Seems he hates me and Orris the most them times. Isn't him, you know! Is the rum."

"Hitting is wrong, rum or no rum!"

"Can't do nothing about it."

"Run to Todd's house with Orris if Leroy gets mean. And Orris can always safely be at school during the week. When he wakes up, please send him my way. No matter he is late. He has an excused tardiness."

Pearl's voiced quivered. She balled her hands together tightly, her thumbs jutting up and touching her chin. "My *husband* told me I had to keep him in the shed all day. No school!"

"You tell your *husband* that *I* said Orris needs to be in school! Any problem with that, he can come to me. Or write to the school director."

Pearl laughed a bit insanely then, eyes darting to and fro like her son's had on his first day of school.

"Leroy don't know how to write!" she nearly shrieked.

"Well then, he can come to me. Remember to say I came by

and you did as you were told. Children are supposed to be in school. Remember, compulsory—required—education is the law."

Pearl nodded so vigorously she reminded me of my students.

"I will tell him now."

"No, let him sleep."

Too late. Pearl shook the boy, his eyes widening when he saw me. "Orris, Orris! Teacher Gale came for you. Required education is the law!"

Orris swung himself up and around in one movement, feet slamming onto the floor with a *thump* before he jumped up, straight as a board, hands by his sides. Despite the bruise that surrounded one of them, his eyes brightened as he checked his nails to find them clean enough. Pearl thrust a lunch basket into my hands, and we left the house.

Up the road, I glanced back to see Pearl leaning on the inside of her doorway with the rotting trim, rubbing her eyes with a dirty white handkerchief. She dropped the kerchief and ran toward us. She knelt, wrapped her arms around Orris, and kissed him on the cheek opposite the black eye.

Pearl looked up and said, "You know, maybe you need to keep Orris after school for a bit? To make up for him being late?"

Orris's silent eyes pleaded as he said, "We think Pop will come home around four o'clock today."

I looked from mother to son. "Seems like we could get good schoolwork done by you staying until five o'clock, young man. Wait, my dear Pearl, will you be all right?"

Orris looked to his mother, took her hand in his two.

"I will." She let Orris go and added firmly, "Keep him in school."

Orris hugged her tight.

Pearl tousled her boy's hair and gently pushed him toward me. He reached out and held my hand.

Irv, Sam, and Lucy stood and clapped as we walked in, the screen door slamming behind us.

"Okay, children, recess for all if we can finish our writing lessons by eleven o'clock!"

Orris dove into his seat next to Lucy. She sat down, pointed to her left eye, scrunched up her face, and mouthed, *Ouch*.

Orris shrugged his shoulders and mouthed, *It's okay*.

27

"Would you walk with me, Orris? I need to stop by the Bell Farm for some of those luscious fall tomatoes they have growing. I will be going right by your house and could use your company."

"Okay."

Orris did not take my hand then and I was glad. Too many people about at five in the afternoon, fishermen home, wives getting dinner ready—except me, for I was late. I counted on Thaddeus tending to his gear, something he often did before his bath.

"Orris?"

"Yes, ma'am?"

"What interests you the most?"

"I dunno."

His eyes fixed on the grassy road. Some of the weeds towered above him. He liked walking straight through it all, pushing stalks to each side with his arms. This explained why his legs, arms, and clothing had been covered with dew the previous morning.

"Really? There must be something. Let's start with what you are not interested in," I said as he disappeared into a thick batch of weeds.

"Writing. Don't like to write one bit!"

"Okay."

"Fishing. Hate fishing. Don't tell my pop!"

"Some things are confidential between teacher and student," I called to the weeds.

"Confi...dential?"

"Means a thought not shared with others. Like something the pupil enjoys studying or doing. Or if he needs to tell the teacher something to help make him safe."

Orris reappeared, scuffled his feet.

"Don't like Pop hitting my ma none."

"You tried to stop him."

Thick tears slid down the boy's face, splashing on a rock. "Didn't do no good. He just hit her harder. And then me."

I squatted, looking into fiery, tearful brown eyes.

"Your ma knows you tried. She is trying to protect you, too. That's her job, you know."

"She can't protect me. She is too small!"

"So are you."

Orris frowned hard. "I am not!"

"Too small and young to go up against your pop, is what I meant. You are not too small for your age."

"Not too young."

"Okay."

My legs hurt too much squatting like that and I got up. We continued at a stroll, both of us slowing the pace on purpose.

"I like the stars."

"The stars?"

"Teacher Gale, you asked what I liked. I like the stars! So many of them. They make patterns. They move around, they do, but stay the same, too! Last year I drew them all once a month. Now I look at the pictures on the same dates, only a year later, and the stars are in the same places!"

"That's because of something called stellar aberration, proven in 1725 by a smart fella like you, James Bradley. From here, looks like the stars are moving, but it is really the earth that is moving around the sun. We learned that about the sun and earth a long time ago, but Mr. Bradley figured out why the stars look the way they do over the course of a year. How about that, young-not-small Orris, Astrono-mer Extraordinaire!"

"You sure talk funny, Mrs. Gale!"

"I know. Talking funny is a teacher's prerogative."

"Don't know what you just said, but I like the stuff about Mr. Bradley."

We ambled along, speaking of the stars and sky. I wished for a longer chat, but too soon said, "We are at your house, Orris. You will be all right then, tonight?"

"Yes, everything is quiet now, so it will be quiet all night."

"That's good. Why is that?"

"Don't know. Just is. If Pa don't start in, you know, with the, um, drink, he falls asleep right after supper, tired from fishing. That's what usually happens."

"Good, then. See you tomorrow in school, on time, with clean nails."

"Yes, ma'am!"

The Jennings front door creaked as Pearl slipped her slender arm through the crack of the entry. She grasped her son's shirt with a single ghostly hand and pulled him into the house as she whispered, "Thank you."

My thoughts filled with hope for that smart little boy and his mother were interrupted by my husband.

"MIIIILLLLLLL-DRED!"

Thaddeus stood on our yard across the harbor, hands on his hips.

"HOME!" he ordered.

I trotted across the mudflats, hating how losing more of my-self felt.

28

"It's past five thirty! What you doing over there?"

"Tomatoes," I answered between gasps of breath. "I wanted tomatoes."

"School ends at four."

"I know, but—"

"But what?"

"Orris. He stayed after school for being late. Not as punishment, but to help him catch up. We left the classroom at five and I walked him home."

"Why was he late?"

"Leroy hit him, Pearl, too."

"Goddamn him! So, Leroy goes off on his family and I'm left here with a late bath and supper. I come first, Mildred. First!"

"But poor little Orris, he needed me!"

"No buts! Me first is how it's got to be."

"Yes, Thaddeus," I agreed, boiling up inside.

"My bath."

"Yes, Thaddeus."

"Go."

With clenched jaw and equally tight heart, I obeyed.

After a great breath and a sigh, I fumed so ferociously while preparing His Majesty's bath in the barn that I spoke out loud. "That man talks constantly about how important children are to Hale Harbor's very survival! And I cannot take care of them the way I should? The way they deserve? I must be home? For his goddamn bath?"

I continued to seethe and curse as I started supper in the kitchen while Thaddeus bathed. In minutes, the Combs in me rose up, and I barged back outside, across the lawn, into the barn. "Thaddeus!"

The man eyed me warily. His arms rested on the sides of the metal tub as he chewed on the final butt end of a lit stogie, its pungent smell mixing with the fragrance of a soapy bath.

I waited, arms crossed.

"Don't you have supper to make?"

"Supper can wait. This cannot."

He groaned, took a deep breath, and slid underwater. I had filled the tub generously, just the way he liked it. Water spilled over, along with the extinguished cigar riding on soap bubbles.

I tapped him on the head just below the surface, noticing with some humor that his privates, buoyed by the water, bounced about. "Stop your shenanigans!"

No response. He became still, as if not moving meant he was invisible.

I threw his dirty and clean clothes into two heaps outside the barn door. If we were going to have a fight, I wanted him trapped so we could finish it.

He stayed underwater.

I tapped again.

He rose, his dark hair matted over his eyes. After a breath, he said, "What in hell do you want from me, Mildred May? Can't a man have a moment's peace?"

"Not when I have no peace of my own. Do not ever call me 'home' across the water for all to hear, like I am some kind of dog."

"You've got no business being over there that time of day."

"I was bringing Orris home and on my way to buy tomatoes— for you! For your bacon, lettuce, and tomato sandwiches."

"I was home. Home wasn't ready for me."

"Thaddeus, good lord, you managed before we were married, why can I not have an hour at the Bell Farm?"

"'Why can I not?' What kind of language is that?"

"Do not change the subject."

"Speak English then."

"I am."

"Don't sound it to me."

"Stop acting like a child!"

"I'm not."

I took my own deep breath, and then exhaled. "Thaddeus!"

"What?!"

"You need to give me freedom to roam around."

"Roam around?"

"Yes. The Bells'. Uptown. Preacher Cove. Maybe even Gooseneck. My, I have never been out to that harbor's edge just right there." I pointed to the west side through the barn window, along the beach, which surely led to a majestic lookout to open ocean.

"You may roam around Hale Harbor. No point going to them other places. You ever see them coming here? Stuck-up creatures they are."

"Why is that?"

"Why are they stuck-up? Just because they are."

"No, why not let me see other parts of the island?"

"Hale is everything. Nothing elsewhere."

I sighed. We were making little progress.

"Why do they not...that is, why don't those other harbor folk ever come around Hale?"

"Once in a while they do. Usually to buy from the Bells. Sometimes even for lobsters from me. But everyone is busy, Mildred May. No time for gallivanting about. Think this is a holiday island, do you?"

"No, but a little time to explore would be nice."

"Maybe in the spring."

"The spring?"

"The spring."

He farted. Bubbles rose to the surface of the water.

I snorted.

"That means I'm hungry. And don't be using so much wood while you cook. Got a whole winter to get through, you know."

"Breaking wind does not mean you are hungry, but I am going anyway, your Royal Highness, to cook. No yelling across the harbor at me. I mean that, Thaddeus, treating me polite is mandatory."

"What in hell does *mandatory* mean?"

"*Mandatory* means *must*."

"Mandatory. Must. No yelling across the harbor at you. Got it."

"Exactly that," and then I added, cringing as the words he did not deserve slipped out, "thank you."

He farted again.

I turned, retrieved his fresh clothes, and dropped them by the tub.

29

A little after four the next afternoon, I took an appreciative breath
while entering Bell's farm on the eastern peninsula. The beauty of
their land, surrounded on three sides by water and dotted with sheep,
cattle, vegetable gardens, and blueberry fields, were unmatched by
anything I had ever seen.

I picked out the four largest tomatoes on Flora's porch table and
told her, "Thaddeus and I are having a party Saturday night for everyone in the harbor. I am making a big batch of lobster chowder. And
baking my mama's chocolate sourdough cake. Food and fun. We are
inviting everyone. Thaddeus insists you bring your fiddle."

Flora burst into such a wide grin, deep lines appeared about her
eyes. "How divine! Everyone? Even Leroy?"

"Why yes, I thought—we thought—to invite all. Naturally, I
want Pearl there. And we cannot very well invite Pearl and not her
husband."

"Mix Leroy's rum with water. Might keep him behaved a bit
longer. Then again, might not help at all. Best just make sure all those
big fishermen are ready to sit on him when he gets out of hand."

"When, not if?"

"When."

"And to think Maine was the first state to ban the sale of alcohol!"

"That never works on the islands."

"I suppose you are right. Oh dear, Flora, I am late. This visit is so pleasant, but I should go. Thank you for the tomatoes. The plumpest I have ever seen. Saturday night will come right quick. Remember your fiddle!"

30

Clypeasteroida, a burrowing sea urchin, more commonly known as a "sand dollar"

"Mildred, you are something. The kitchen smells like heaven!"

"Thank you, Thaddeus. Best lobster in the world makes the best chowder."

"Smells more than lobster. What you got in there?"

I dipped a metal ladle into the simmering white broth and held it to his mouth, proud of my potato, lobster, and rosemary-dill concoction.

"Try to tell me what herbs I used."

Thaddeus pressed his lips to the ladle and then jumped back. "Ach! Goddamn you, Mildred!!"

I started to wipe the cream off his chin. He swatted my wrist!

"Jesus, you are some stupid!"

With a shaking hand, I ladled broth into a mug on the counter. And tried to control a galloping heart. Nobody had ever called me stupid.

Maybe marrying you *was stupid*, I wanted to say.

Thaddeus left the kitchen and stomped up the stairs, swearing under his breath.

Mercifully, I then heard giggles, and the schooner bell attached to the outside wall dinged sharply. Two bright faces peeked inside the door, one head bobbing above the other.

I welcomed the Thomas brothers with "Raspberries in the dining room!"

The boys skedaddled through the kitchen to the treats. I served those berries fresh on the vine set in the middle of the table.

"Eve, so nice to see you. Is Irville coming with his mandolin?"

"He's on his way. Getting cleaned up, is all. Seems the men had a rough day of it out there this afternoon. That husband of mine is in a foul mood."

"What happened?"

"Don't know exactly, Irville doesn't always give me the skinny on everything on the water. Kind of irritating, actually."

I nodded. "I know how you feel."

Eve continued, "Maybe Leroy and Jon have been poaching some again, or that's what our men think. Those three could just be catching less and blaming it on someone else."

"Could be. And unless a poacher is caught red-handed, there is not much anyone can do about it."

"That's right. I wish they'd all get along. Always something. I mean, not many people down here in this little hole of a harbor. We need to get on more fine."

"Well said. Honestly Eve, us all getting along is partly why I wanted to have this party. I hope everyone comes. Made my grandma's chowder for it."

As I mentioned the main course, a lump formed in my throat. *Damn that Thaddeus!* He had just about ruined my evening before it had even started.

"Smells absolutely delicious! What's in it?"

"Try some. Rosemary's the secret."

I handed Eve the cup of soup. "Careful, it might still be hot."

Eve brought the dark-brown mug to her lips, eyes on me. "Ohhhhhh my, this is delicious! I can taste the rosemary. And dill. And potatoes. And butter. Good thing you have a giant pot of this."

"Going outside," announced Irv Junior to his mother as he bounded into the kitchen with Sam, their lips and cheeks a rosy red from the wild berries mushed into their mouths.

"Don't get dirty." Eve winked at her sons.

The boys ran between Rufus Mank and Todd Calderwood on their way up the porch steps. Eve glanced my way, a mischievous smile on her face, perhaps noticing the stark contrast between them. Mank, the much shorter of the two, looked as he always did, a disheveled, dirty mess. He was still wearing the same clothes he had on the first day I arrived—and every day since then, far as I could tell.

Mank looked at his tattered shoes. "Afternoon."

"Good afternoon! Come on in, Mr. Mank, and Mr. Calderwood. We are so glad you could make it."

Todd pulled an oversized bouquet of flowers out from behind his back, their colors vivid against his crisp white shirt.

I nearly ripped them out of his hand. "Todd, thank you. Are these from your garden, or did you pick them from the wild?"

"My garden."

Eve grinned as she watched me turn the flowers side-to-side.

"I recognize the Lemon Queen Helianthus, but what are these pink ones?"

"Cosmos. I wanted something to complement the yellow sunflowers with what deer don't eat. I've tried irises before, unsuccessfully. I didn't know if Cosmos would take, but, well, seems they did just fine, maybe because they are also of the sunflower family. You like them?"

"Lovely, simply lovely."

Thaddeus walked in then. He had changed his shirt into one of my favored double-breasted flannel style, the forest-green one with gray buttons. He took my free hand, the one he had slapped, raised it, and kissed the back.

"Goodness me!" Eve gasped. Todd stepped aside, a wide smile on his blushing face.

I was so mad at Thaddeus! To act so proper, in front of everybody, after being so mean to me just minutes before.

"Nice flowers," my husband said, extending his hand to Todd for a shake.

Soon everyone arrived. Everyone! Lucy, Orris, and brothers Sam and Irv ran about the beach looking for sand dollars. Flora, Pearl, Eve, and Min gathered in the kitchen with me. Thaddeus put

117

a pack of cards in his shirt pocket and grabbed four bottles of rum, two in each hand. With a commanding nod he led the men out and onto the porch. Those boys squeezed in around the tiny round table, Thaddeus next to Irville and Marvin.

The rest of us stood in the warm kitchen leaning against the cherry countertops, except for Flora, who peered through the window at the men. "I have never, ever seen every single Hale Harbor fellow together! Wish that Ellsworth photographer wedding couples use was here to document such a historic event."

"Maybe an honest game of cards will do them boys some good," added Eve.

"Let's hope so."

"Could happen," added Min. "Mildred, do you know about Rufus yet?"

"No, I do not," I replied, feeling uncomfortable with how quickly we began talking about Hale's own. None of the women could say anything about the others' husbands, leaving Rufus Mank and Todd Calderwood our prime subjects.

"Word is Mank got mixed up in something nasty over there in Rockland when he was just a kid—bank thieving, a stabbing, not sure what all else. Served seven years in some kind of plea deal including snitching on his partner, a right vicious man from Texas. That fella was sentenced to twenty-seven years in a Maine slammer up north by the Canadian border. People say Mank's scared to death the Texan's friends will catch up with him, so Rufus—or whatever his name is—changed his name and is hiding out here."

"My oh my!"

"Who'd ever name a baby 'Rufus Mank' anyway, got to be made up," Min continued.

Added Eve, "He don't seem to do much, just don't know how he lives on the wee bit of fishing, and here-and-there handy work he gets. Maybe Rufus still has some of that bank money buried in his backyard."

Pearl laughed.

"You don't think so, Pearl?" asked Eve.

"I...ah..." Pearl stuttered, "Is fun to think about. Buried treasure. On a little island."

"We should all have buried treasure," decided Mineola, turning to the soup. Tiny bubbles popped on its surface. She took an exaggerated sniff. "Then we could stay at some dang fine hotel and do some dang nice shopping on Saks Fifth Avenue. That's what I'd like. And that's what we deserve for putting up with those card-dealing, rum-sucking, bait-stinking fellas twelve months of the year."

The gals in my kitchen laughed in agreement.

"Tell me about Mr. Calderwood. He seems a fine fellow. He sure does dress nicely."

More snickers.

"I said something funny?"

My new friends looked at each other, eyes sparkling as playfully as young girls talking about their first kiss.

"Oh, come now, it could not be that bad. Todd certainly is not a criminal. Someone tell me what you are chuckling about."

Min punched Eve's arm lightly. "You tell her, Eve."

"Well okay, if I have to," Eve replied, clearly thrilled with the assignment. "We all adore Todd, but, well, he's been here for years. Never seen him with the female sort."

"Not a one?"

"Nope."

"And his house. And clothes." Pearl was blushing and breathless.

"That's right," continued Min, "way too clean. Lovely, actually. You just saw him—that lovely graying hair and new beard of his so neatly combed, and wearing a nice shirt and tie, pressed dress slacks. Even his shoes are polished to a blinding shine. The man always looks good, even when working."

"What's wrong with combing your hair and wearing nice clothes?"

"He's a carpenter. Not natural to look good while slamming nails," Min answered.

"You ask me, nails aren't all he's slamming."

Flora gasped. "Eve, my word! You been nipping some of that rum?"

Pearl covered her mouth with one hand, eyes as big as saucers. "Are you all saying he is sweet on fellows? I do not believe it."

"Believe it, Mildred," replied Eve.

"You have proof?"

"What kind of proof you want?"

"Well now, I am not sure, a boyfriend maybe? Has a man ever come out here to visit Todd who seemed, well, you know, more than a friend?"

"You get right to the point, don't you, Mildred," observed Min.

"Truly now, an obvious boyfriend would be the only almost kind of proof, right?"

"He goes on trips." Pearl's voice became high-pitched. "To Portland!"

"Maybe his girlfriend is there."

"Or his boyfriend."

Eve stopped talking, eyes darting right as Thaddeus barged in.

"Mildred dear, got any of them lip-smacking donuts and cheese for us? Have quite a card game going. Need something to keep *us* going."

The women stood still as granite, hands neatly at their sides.

"Here you go, Thaddeus. Do not eat too many or you will all spoil your appetites for supper."

Thaddeus took the plate and picked up a warm, brown donut from the top of the pile. "Mmmm-*mmm*! Not eating too many of these is going to be hard, my good wife, but we'll try."

The women breathed a collective sigh as the door closed.

Mineola watched Thaddeus through the window as he returned to the game. "Mildred, you sure got yourself a wonderful fella there."

Added Eve, "Thought he'd never marry. Thaddeus's heart be wrapped around you something big. How'd you do it?"

"Well, honestly, I do not know."

"Try," ordered Eve.

"Well, Thaddeus showed up at the boatyard on Crescent Island one day. I was there, too, searching for my pa. Thaddeus was looking at a dory. The following Sunday, he rowed over again."

"What did you talk about?" asked Pearl.

"Boats, I think."

"Anything else?" asked Flora.

"The weather perhaps."

"Well that's it, then!" decided Min. "A fisherman's two favorite subjects. Boats and weather landed you on his dance card, kicking any other prospects off the floor."

I smiled at my friends and dragged the big pot to the edge of the stove to let it cool. But in that blessed, peaceful moment, the house shuddered as all hell broke loose on the porch.

31

Thaddeus and Leroy stood face-to-face, fists clenched. Blood dripped from Leroy's chin. Two chairs lay sideways on the porch deck. The rest of the men pressed themselves along the railings or walls, giving the fighters room. Young Jon Jennings looked like he might cry.

"MISTER GALE!"

"You stay out of this, woman!" Thaddeus growled as he feigned a punch at Leroy.

Leroy took a heavy, lopsided swing, missed, and staggered left.

Eve crossed her arms as hard as her face was stern. I stood between Todd and Eve.

Todd wrung his hands. "They are both three sheets to the wind, I'm afraid."

Eve shook her finger at her husband. "Do something, Irville, for goodness sake!"

"You stay out of this, too, Eve," Irville said less forcefully than Thaddeus. "Leroy's been poaching Thaddeus's pots. Said so himself. Kind of a stupid son of a bitch to brag about it."

Thaddeus let out a deep cackle and pushed Leroy. Leroy's head snapped back, hitting the white-painted porch post with a sharp *thwonk*.

Eve tried again. "That's the rum talking! Maybe he hasn't poached at all. He likes riling Thaddeus, you know that."

"Stay out of this, I said!"

"Don't tell me to stay out of nothing!"

"Is true about the poaching," Jon whispered, voice shaking as he spoke to Eve and me. "Very sorry."

I glanced at Jon and nodded. Gently touched his arm.

Thaddeus hulked over Leroy, letting Leroy swing about a bit more, then grabbed him by the back of the shirt collar and pants. As Marv, Irv, and Rufus scattered, Thaddeus ran Leroy across the porch and threw him over the railing as if he were just a giant rag doll.

Thaddeus leaned over the rail and thrust his fist into the air. "I dare you come near my traps again! Gives me a damn good reason to kill you. And I'd sure like killing you a whole lot!"

Jennings groaned once, and then settled, still as the air. Todd gave Jennings a concerned glance, but other than that, each man, including young Jon, seated himself and scooped up the playing cards and continued their game.

Leroy's little Orris dashed up the porch steps, jumping into his mother's arms so hard she staggered back, Flora steadying Pearl so she and her son would not fall. Too heavy for her, Pearl let Orris slide gently to the floor. She then wrapped her spindly arms around his back and head, pulling him into her stomach while she stroked his hair. She cupped his chin in two hands and kissed his creased forehead.

"Show's over!" Min announced to the women. "The children's hermit crab beach races are about to start. Come on, Pearl, Orris, let's go."

I searched for Todd's attention and mouthed, *Is he breathing?*

Todd looked to his right at Thaddeus peering into his cards with bloodshot eyes, glanced over the railing, and gave me a single slow, reassuring nod.

32

Hermit crab

Down by the low-tide mark, Pearl grasped my arm and buried her head above my elbow. We had just watched Leroy pull himself up off the ground, and with a wave of his arm command Jon to follow. Jon struggled to keep up with his father on the beach, even as Leroy veered left and right. As Leroy staggered past Lucy and Orris crouching behind a rock, Jon raised his finger to his mouth, signaling them to be quiet. Orris clutched his race-winning hermit crab to his chest as Lucy put her arm around him, pulling him tight.

I touched Pearl on the arm.

"Do not worry, my dear Pearl. Leroy's so liquored up, he'll just go home and sleep it off."

She gripped my arm harder.

The moment Leroy entered their house, Pearl released her grip.

"I'm hungry." announced Samuel.

"Sam, don't be so impolite," ordered his mother.

"Well, he surely must be famished by now," I agreed, relieved to think about something else.

Watching Lucy holding Orris's hand as we all walked to the house, I shared, "When the time comes, Thaddeus wants a boy, but I am wishing for a girl."

"You have a girl," agreed Flora. "That'd make us four boys and two girls in the harbor, if Jon still counts as a young'un."

"He counts."

"Jon is a good boy," Pearl added. "Sweet, he is. Leroy makes him do bad things. Oh no! Please don't tell your husbands I said that."

Eve squeezed Pearl on the shoulder. "We'll not say a thing. We gals take care of each other, remember?"

As we got to the edge of the shore below the house, Thaddeus slammed his cards down so hard, an empty bottle of rum toppled off the table with a clatter.

"I win! You all lose! Time for chowder!"

Though they could not see his winning hand, no one argued.

"Getting brisk out here. We will eat inside."

No one argued with me, either.

33

Todd picked up two chairs and followed Thaddeus, who held the table with one hand, a chair in the other. Irville, Marvin, and Miles picked up the rest. Rufus looked about, shrugged, and walked into the house empty-handed.

Rufus sniffed the kitchen air. "Smells something good. That the chowder?"

"The best." Thaddeus winked at me.

I ignored my husband. "Not formal here. Line up with a bowl, youngest to oldest, but we do not need to be too exact about it. Children first, is all."

Everyone lined up in close order: Lucy, Orris, Samuel, Irville Junior, then Rufus, Pearl, Min, Eve, Flora, Miles, Irville Senior, Marvin, and Todd. Thaddeus pulled in last even though he was younger than Marv and Todd. I was glad he was being so polite to our guests.

I ladled myself a big bowl after Thaddeus.

"Mmm-*mmm*," said Mank. "Best dang soup I've ever had."

"Why thank you, Rufus. Try bread with it. Eve's specialty rye."

Rufus slid three pieces onto his plate with his soupspoon.

Dusk settling in, the light of the oil lamps flickered off Orris's face as he sat cross-legged on the floor next to the Thomas brothers. The three young boys sat by the potbelly stove, gulping up their chowder as if someone was about to take it away. Lucy sat beside them, staring at her bowl as if in prayer.

All was quiet in that corner of the room except for the low growl of the fire, spoons clanking on the sides of bowls, and satisfied slurps.

Mank let out a deep burp, the children giggled, and I announced, "Plenty more chowder!"

"Anyone has less than seconds be a darn fool and won't be invited back," said Thaddeus, looking around the table, pretending to be stern.

Thaddeus then went to the kitchen, returning with the oversized pot. "She's hot, watch out!"

With a *thud* he placed the pot on a large trivet. He then served up a last round for everyone.

Marvin leaned back in his chair and patted his stomach. "That is some soup, by God, but I can't manage another bite."

Thaddeus ignored him, dangling and circling the dripping ladle toward Marvin. Marvin came forward, chair landing hard, and placed his hand over his bowl. Thaddeus poured anyway, thick chunks of potato and creamy pieces of lobster sliding between Marv's fingers into the bowl.

I was some grateful the chowder had cooled down by then.

Soon the four little ones curled up together and fell asleep like puppies in a litter. Something about warm milk after a long day... I, too, felt like I could nod off right there on the floor with the children.

When the women began clearing the table, I did not object, only stood up to help. Soon we were in the kitchen, dishes stacked high by the sink.

I closed the door between rooms.

I playfully pushed Eve aside. "Eve, dishwashing is my job."

She pushed me back as gently. "Absolutely not."

"I am the hostess. My kitchen."

"You're not doing the dishes. Not staying on your feet another second."

"What are you talking about?"

Eve smiled, glanced at Mineola and nodded. "You be right, Min. New girl just don't know her own self! How hilarious."

"Do not know what?"

Eve turned around, dirty plate in hand, back to the sink. "Shall I tell her?"

"Tell me what?"

"You tell her, Eve," agreed Min.

"Mildred, as sure as the sun comes up in the east, you are pregnant!"

Flora's eyes sparkled. Min laughed. Pearl clapped her hands.

Min continued where Eve had left off. "Let me ask, to be even more sure: when was your last cycle?"

"I guess, um—my oh my, it is late!"

Eve beamed at me. "'Course it's late. Look at your breasts. Huge, they are."

Pearl squealed.

I looked down. They had been bulging out of my brassiere lately. I just could not figure out why, because other than that, it seemed I had lost weight.

"This...this is so fast. We've only been together a few months."

"Babies been made faster than that, my dear," Min said. "At least you're married."

Min winked at Eve, who faked a scowl. "Mineola Browne, why I never!"

I hugged Min, then Eve, Flora, and Pearl—and missed my ma something so very fierce.

"Thank you for telling me. I guess I did not know."

"You would have figured it out soon enough," said Flo.

"Yes," added Min.

"I am happy. And nervous. This is a lot to take in."

"Don't you worry none," said Min. "We'll get Doc Hornby to see you along the way. And Eve here helped Flora the night Lucy was born. She'll do that again, won't you, Eve?"

"Can hardly wait!"

"I need to sit down."

I wanted everyone to leave so I could be alone with Thaddeus. I was glad music seemed to have dropped from the evening's agenda.

Pearl was the first to go that evening, scooping up a sleeping Orris and trying to carry him. Too heavy, she said gently, "Wake up, Orris."

The boy opened his eyes. "I like it here, Mommy. Can we stay?"

Pearl brushed his bangs aside. "No, sweetheart, this is not our home."

Then she whispered in his ear, "Pop will be asleep, I promise."

Orris got up and held her hand. Pearl hugged me tight before they went out the door.

Min took Marvin's hand. "Come on, my fella. Let's go have our own evening now!"

"Remember what we talked about," Thaddeus said to Marvin, ignoring guests still standing at the door. "Can't take no chances out there with our gear."

"Won't forget. No way, no how."

"Good, has to be done."

"I know."

"What a lovely time! Thank you!" Flora held her unused fiddle in one hand, the other on Lucy's shoulder as she slept in Miles's arms.

"Very much our pleasure, isn't that right, Thaddeus?"

Thaddeus blinked. "'Course. Hope to see you again soon. Don't see much of you, being so far way over there on the peninsula."

"Come by the farm some time," invited Miles.

"Well then, I might just do that."

"Eve, you take the boys home, I'll be right up," said Irville.

"Irville Thomas! Thaddeus and Mildred need their evening."

Barely able to stand, I was so exhausted, I mouthed Eve a thank-you for her protest. I could not wait to tell Thaddeus he would be a father!

But Thaddeus slurred, "Irville's staying, got some chatting still to do."

Eve frowned. "You fellas hit the rum again while we cleaned up, didn't you?"

"A little," confessed Irville.

Eve shrugged and roused her boys. I followed them out the back door.

"Mildred dear, you kick my Irv out when you want him to go. He and Thaddeus could stay up all night."

"I will leave them be and go to bed."

"Good for the baby, that."

Young Irville rubbed his eyes. "What baby?"

"Never you mind, Irv Junior," Eve said, patting his head. "Let's go boys."

34

Four thirty a.m. Thaddeus stirred. I rolled to one side and out of bed.

"Don't go, Mildred."

"Got to get breakfast on."

"There's time."

"Not much."

"Enough. I need you. Real hard for me to admit that, you know."

"I know."

I pulled the sleeve of my white nightie off my left shoulder.

"Good God!" Thaddeus jumped out of bed.

I knew my breasts were magnificent, could hardly believe them myself.

"What the hell happened to you?" He grabbed my wrist, yanking my bare arm straight up. "Them bruises, how the hell did you get them?"

"Thaddeus, that hurts!"

"How'd you get them?!"

His grip tightened.

"Stop it and I will tell you!"

He dropped my arm. I pulled my sleeve back up.

Thaddeus sat back on the bed. "Am listening."

"Last evening, when Leroy staggered home across the beach, Pearl held on to me, she did. Poor girl had no idea how tightly she had my arm, was some nervous. I did not realize either. Is nothing."

"Damn son of a bitch. Jennings has no business living. He roughs Pearl and that boy up, and now you have bruises, too. Everyone'll think I did that!"

"I will tell the world, I will, you did not. Why are you so worked up? Look how small the marks are. Such a tiny hand Pearl has."

"Am saying it again, Leroy Jennings has no business living."

"Well, you cannot do anything about that."

"The hell I can't."

"Thaddeus, how ridiculous. What are you insinuating?"

"Speak English."

"What do you mean by what you just said about Leroy?"

"Nothing. You just wear long sleeves, I tell you. Don't let nobody see them bruises. Don't want no one thinking I did that."

"Bruises will be gone in a couple of days. Poor little Pearl, and Orris, they are the ones we should worry about."

"Well, you be right about that, Mildred. Sorry my voice was so... so rough. Don't like seeing you bruised up."

"I am all right. Thaddeus, I thought you were going to make love to me."

He grinned. I loved how I could just say that, and he melted, big man, king of the seas, becoming downright helpless.

"Oh yes, I can do that. Going to get you pregnant, I am."

"You have already done that."

Thaddeus did not move, face a frozen stare. Slowly, a wide grin formed. And his eyes brightened. "I was right again. Always am! Knew you could do it, right proud of you, Mildred."

"Well, took the two of us."

"That's right. And now that I got you pregnant, everyone'll know it's not my family's fault. Leaves Min."

"Thaddeus!"

"Min or Marv or both, don't care, we be way ahead of them already."

"Having babies is not a competition. And why me? Why not any of those other women you tried on?"

"You know about them."

"Yes."

"They stayed at the Brownes'. Min must have told you that."

"She did."

The wind howled as I waited for him to say more, gusts forcing their way through window frames, blowing my nightie against my legs and slamming the bedroom door shut.

"Why didn't you test me out like them, let me have a go here in the harbor before getting engaged?"

"Trying women out wasn't working. None of them liked it down here. Plus, we were running out of time."

"We or you?"

"Both. All of us."

"I did not marry the community."

"You did."

"Well, Mr. Know-it-all Gale, how could you be sure I would like it here?"

"Wasn't. So I married you first. Earned you, too, by Jesus, rowing all that way to Crescent so many times. And I do know it all, by the way, you got that part right."

"Why are you so full of yourself?"

"Because there ain't no one better."

"Thaddeus, you are *so* full of yourself!"

"You are pregnant now, can't go nowhere, no how."

"My word!"

"Just telling you like it is."

"You love this harbor more than you love me!"

I clenched my fists and held them behind me, like Irville had done the day Orris was in the shed. I was as angry with myself as I was with Thaddeus, for getting myself into a fight instead of early-morning romance.

"Think what you want, Mildred."

"And you needed me here so the school would not close."

"You don't like your job?"

135

"That is not the point."

"We needed you, Mildred, what's wrong with that?"

"Need is not love."

"We talking about this again? Anyway, is close."

"Not in my book."

"Maybe this here harbor ain't got the luxury of your book."

"You said you loved me, before!"

"Do I have to say it all the time?"

"You do not love me all the time?"

"Well, enough of the time, yes."

"Thaddeus!"

"What?"

"I need to be loved, all the time, not needed, all of the time."

"Well, that's funny. I need to be needed all the time. Don't right understand the love part. Makes me mighty uncomfortable."

I turned my back, crossed my arms.

"Mildred."

"Just never you mind! You tricked me into getting married. You tricked me into getting pregnant!"

I ran downstairs.

By the time I reached the living room, he was there, gripping my arm on top of my bruise. I screamed in pain.

"That's right!" Thaddeus yelled above shrieking wind, his face so close his spit spattered my cheek. "Was up to me! Who'd marry that Rufus 'Stank'? And Todd Calderwood? Never seen him with a woman, never even seen him look at a woman. He's probably one of those. Was up to me. *I* needed to save the harbor!"

"Stop hurting me! And stop maligning Todd!"

"Wish you'd speak more English."

"*Maligning* means say bad things about."

"Figured that by context, that word you taught me before."

"Let go!"

He let go.

Thaddeus put his head in his hands and moaned, "Damn it, Mildred! *You* made me grab you like that. Don't ever do that to me again. Don't. Don't. Don't."

"*You* don't," I barely whispered.

"It is not that easy not to... I, goddamn it, you have no idea!"

He started crying.

Weeping and wailing.

Like Otto's mother had at her only child's funeral.

35

How could the toughest fisherman on the coast be full-on blubbering like that? Had he not hurt me, I would have felt sorry for Thaddeus. Would have sat right down and wrapped my arms around him.

Instead I walked away.

He sobbed for an hour, alone in the living room, as I sat at the kitchen table overlooking the harbor, watching and feeling my arm turn red around the initial bruise. It would become even more black and blue in a few days. I changed out of my nightie into a long-sleeved dress hanging on the drying rack by the woodstove. I washed the rug the children had soaked with spilled chowder.

When he became silent, I set three fried eggs, four strips of bacon, brown bread, butter, and fresh jam on the table. Coffee. Lots of coffee.

"Thaddeus, come eat," I called to the next room.

No answer. I entered the living room. He took my extended hand. I led him to our table, me sitting in his usual spot, nearest the door. With each mouthful, the color came back into his face and he seemed to relax. Still, I readied myself to run outside if he snapped.

Another gulp of coffee and he set down the mug. When he

finally spoke, his voice was tempered. Weeping seemed to have done him good.

"Don't go telling the women about me crying like that."

"I would not."

"I did trick you, Mildred, I sure did."

"Being tricked is disappointing."

"I know, but there's more."

"Is it bad?"

"No. Good. I think it is good. Hope you think so, too."

"Tell me." I enjoyed the unusual feeling of patience, and hope.

"I lied to you, I did. More like, kept the truth to myself. Made a big sacrifice, too, since I did not really know...or love you. You didn't love me, neither! Took me five times asking for you to finally say yes, remember that? And them times on Crescent was all we had to get to know each other. Sure, I tricked you into being here. Sure, I set out to find a schoolteacher. And, well, 'course had to find someone unmarried. I admit all that now. But Mildred, look at us. We're not too bad together. And you are pregnant, after all. That proves one thing, don't it?"

"Proves we have sex."

"You mean more to me than sex, am trying to tell you that."

"Love?"

"Yes, love."

"You didn't love me before, yet you asked. Were there any other reasons you picked me to marry?"

"Well, there is another, kind of, um, yes, a rather a big one."

"Bigger than bringing Hale Harbor more children and keeping the school open?"

"Yes."

"Thaddeus, you must tell me."

"I hope I can someday, Mildred May, I really...really I do. Is why I—" His voice cracked, "—is why I blubbered the hell up like a damn fool!"

"Thaddeus, you should tell me. Would do you, and me, plenty of good."

"Right now I just want to hold you."

He took my arm gently then. "Mildred, I am so very sorry. I will tell you more someday."

"No more tricks, please."

"No more tricks."

I held my arm. "No more hurts."

"I hope not. I will try."

"Try is not good enough. But it is a start toward a promise. I will be needing a promise."

"Mildred, why did you finally say yes?"

"It was November, soon to be December. You were not taking no for an answer, kept showing up to ask again. I did not want you crossing Silver Bay in the death months of winter. Didn't want to be responsible for a man drowning."

"You cared for me, even then."

"Yes, I cared for you, even then. And I care for you now."

The sun settled on its midmorning high before we finally rolled out of bed. We quickly dressed behind the curtained west window, readying for a fall afternoon. Our warm Maine Indian Summer was underway.

I peered out the window at a flat blue harbor and sparkling silver seas beyond. "You are going to have a fine day of it today, dear."

"After what you just did to me, that's for sure."

"I meant the weather."

"I meant you."

He kissed me, his hand resting on my cheek for a moment then sliding down along my neck, over my dress, pressing against my breast. "Your...these...they are glorious!"

"That's the baby coming, Thaddeus, makes breasts go like that."

"I like it."

"So do I."

"You should be pregnant all the time. That's how we'll get ten of them."

"I am going to get as big as a cow everywhere, might be sick some mornings, too. And, for some of the time, later months, that is, we must not...you know. You are a big fella, and we will need to be careful."

"Don't mind. Going to have a boy, we are. Worth the abscess."

"You mean abstinence. My, we really must get on with our reading lessons. You know, we might have a girl."

"Don't think so. A boy, he is."

"A boy, or girl, either is fine."

"Jesus Christ!"

Sighing, I followed Thaddeus's gaze to see Jon Jennings rowing in from the outer harbor, his boat bobbing in the rolls beyond the ledge.

"What's he doing wrong?"

"Bet Leroy sent him out to mess with my pots again, that useless coward! He can't stand my profits, so he nips away at my haul. Tries to catch up by cheating, by stealing, making his own boy do his dirty work."

"Just remember what you just said yourself, that whatever Jon does, is his papa ordering him so. Everyone in the harbor knows that. They will understand if you are easy on the lad."

"I will remember."

Thaddeus put on his boots, grabbed himself hunks of bread and cheese, and set out to confront Jon.

I hummed as I went about my chores. Only four eggs produced by lazy hens. No matter. A messy table left by Thaddeus and Irville the night before. No matter. A pile of sewing to do. No matter. I felt important. I was the teacher, *and* I was going to be a mother!

As I swept the porch, I watched Orris skip in circles above the rocky shore in front of his home, a light northern breeze catching the top of the tall grass he played in. Pearl, usually scurrying about outside that time of day, sat on her porch. Sat! She watched her two sons—Orris in front, Jon with Thaddeus in the harbor—hands neatly folded in her lap.

I, too, watched Jon and Thaddeus. Boats alongside each other, Thaddeus's left hand holding onto Jon's boat, they drifted toward the west side of the harbor as they talked. Thaddeus seemed relaxed. Did Jon just nod? To my surprise, Thaddeus extended his right hand. A man and a boy, in the middle of the harbor, shook hands across the water between their skiffs.

36

For Thaddeus's first reading lesson, we sat at our table by the window overlooking our harbor. By then, the first Sunday in October, twenty rounded lobster traps needing repair lined the shore by the barn.

We started easy, with *Goodnight Moon*.

"What a silly baby story!"

"I know, Thaddeus, but we can use the story to learn to read the words."

"Okay, the baby book will do, just don't go telling nobody."

"I will not."

"Do you know what happened to Leroy?"

"Where'd that come from?"

"I have not seen him for a while."

"Good."

"You do not want to talk about it?"

"Nope."

"What's this one about?" he asked the following week.

Thaddeus had picked up a picture book about a boy and his boat.

"Well, you can see by the drawings. Pictures are your first hint what each page says."

"I'm sick of saying goodnight to the goddamn moon. Read this boat one to me."

He always asked me to read the book out loud, moments I cherished as much as reading stories to the children at school. I would read, and then we would break down each page, each sentence, each word, until he said them all correctly. I expected Thaddeus to be frustrated at times, but he never was. I kept the lesson to an hour and a half, treating my husband just as I did my younger students, stopping when still wanting more.

Thaddeus was my best student, but I could not crow about him one bit.

"I want this one!" Thaddeus held up a large book with a dark-green cover. It was the second to last Sunday of October.

"*The Sea Fairies*? That was just published in 1911. We are so lucky to have this book."

"Them fairies look creepy. I like the sea, though. Reckon it's a fun yarn."

"It's a big book, but we certainly can work on it, page by page."

"Page by page be fine."

"You know, dear, I have been thinking. Maybe we can bring Jon in for reading lessons, too. I don't think he knows how."

"He don't."

"How do you know?"

"Asked him."

"How would you feel about him joining us these Sundays?"

"Then the whole island would know we don't read."

"You do read. You are learning to read more."

"Don't want Jon learning with me. Not yet, anyway."

"All right. Can you ask Jon where his father is?"

"That's none of our business."

"I thought everything in this harbor was our business."

"Learning fast, you are."

"So, am I right, Leroy is our business?"

"You be right. This time, though, just never you mind about it."

"You telling me to never mind makes me want to know what happened even more."

"Got to trust me on this, Mildred."

"I see. I will try not to think about him."

"That's a good girl."

"My name is Mildred. And I am a grown woman."

"Yes, ma'am."

"That's better." I kissed him on the cheek, tried not to think about Leroy, knowing that not wondering would never last.

37

S oon we were almost out of October.

    I was glad for a Saturday, when fishermen came home earlier.

    Thaddeus smelled extra putrid that day. Never could stand bait-fish stink, especially the bottom-of-the-box-pogies-dead-for-a-long-time kind. Herring, at least, were a little sweeter—to me, anyway.

"How about a kiss when I walk in the door?"

Blew him a kiss. He threw his head back as if it hit him. I liked that.

"So, what about Leroy? Still no sign of him."

"You don't quit, do you?"

"Rarely."

"What do the women say?"

"I have been so busy with school, I have not seen much of anybody."

"Not even Min?"

"Not even Min."

"I thought you weren't going to think about Leroy."

"I have tried not to, really I have."

"Don't know what happened to him."

"I do not believe you!"

"I am your husband!"

"I...Thaddeus, I am so sorry. I *do* believe you. I just...well, it makes no sense! Where do you think Leroy went?"

"Does it matter?"

"Yes it matters!"

"What a terrier you are, girl."

"He must be coming back. It would be nice to know when. When I asked Pearl, she shook her head, said nothing."

"Thought you didn't see the women. Thought you weren't going to ask Pearl."

"I said I did not see *much* of the women. I could not stand it, went over there after school yesterday. Her whole house, you know, looks very nice, all clean, Jon fixed the floorboards. It will be a lot warmer now come winter."

"Good."

"And Leroy?"

"He's not coming back."

"Mr. Thaddeus Gale, *what* do you know?"

"Just a hunch, is all. Has Orris said anything at school?"

"No, that sweet boy has not said a word. I have not asked him a thing. I do want to. But it's not right for a teacher to ask a child a question like that. I could try Pearl again, but asking her is of no use, am sure of it. When I spoke to her about Leroy, she got some quiet, and then changed the subject to Orris."

"Never stopped teachers before you from nosing around families through their students. You are a good woman, Mildred, better than most. You do me proud."

"So, we still do not know where Leroy Jennings is."

"You know what I think? I think he just up and left. Wouldn't be the first time a man did that. He said his first wife left him and Jon, but that's just what he said. Maybe he's the leaving one. Maybe he took Jon with him and left that wife high and dry."

"Men do not usually take the children when they leave their wives."

Thaddeus grunted.

I sighed. "You just go wash up, please. You smell worse today than I ever remember. You need a bath before supper. I got some steaks from Rover. He came down today peddling them."

"Better not have paid too much for them."

"Twenty-five cents a pound," I said proudly.

Thaddeus snorted. "Too much. Don't pay no more than twenty-two cents next time."

"Yes, Thaddeus."

Water sloshed from the corner of the living room where we kept the metal tub in colder months, privacy secured by the white lace curtains I had made.

"Mildred May!"

"Yes, Thaddeus."

"My back." An order.

I slapped the steak down on the kitchen counter, went to Thaddeus, picked up the bar of lavender soap, dipped it into the tub water, and began scrubbing his back.

"That feels nice. What would I do without you?"

"Damn well draw your own baths, cook your own suppers, tend the chickens, darn your own socks, sew up your own britches, pick crabs until your fingers cramp up, dig for clams, chisel hundreds of claw pegs, collect mussels, make your own bed, and make love to yourself."

Thaddeus belly-laughed so hard water splashed out of the tub. "You be right about all that, Mildred May, except the love to myself part. I'm not into that way."

"Secretly religious?"

"Nope. Not me. Just don't need that way."

"You are telling me that a virgin man at thirty-five never worked on himself?"

"Mildred, you sure are something to say that!"

"Not going to answer me?"

"Nope."

Using a dark washcloth, I started from the top and worked my way down. Body like his, I could not stay mad for long. I felt my own breathing even out. Thaddeus was fully undressed, and I was not. I could do anything I wanted, and he would be helpless for it. I was thinking of a lot of things.

My thoughts were interrupted by loud banging on the door.

I threw the cloth onto the floor. It splatted even harder than the steak had on the counter.

"My word, who could that be?"

"Someone with bad timing," Thaddeus grumbled.

I opened the door.

Constable Joshua York stood straight and tall. A big man fit for his profession, he was beefy and bald, with wrinkles around his brown eyes and bushy, uneven eyebrows.

I went onto the porch. "Have a seat, Mr. York. What can I do for you?"

"No need, Mrs. Gale, won't be long. Mighty sorry about this, I have come for Mr. Gale."

"Why, whatever for?"

Constable York's eyes never left the weathered gray floorboards as he replied, "For the murder of Leroy Jennings, ma'am. Now go get him, please."

38

"I don't like this any more than you do," Joshua confessed as he handcuffed my husband right there on the porch for all the world to see. Todd stood on the rocky shore of the harbor, looking our way. Flora and Miles watched from their distant porch.

Vexing me further, Thaddeus stood tall, grinning like the Cheshire cat.

"I just do not understand," I said to the constable, surprised at how soft my voice was. I should have been yelling. I wanted to scream.

"I'm not at liberty to say anything more about it. Suggest you find a good attorney."

"I do not know any attorney! They must be expensive!"

Thaddeus kissed me on the cheek. "Mildred, don't you be worrying none. Police have nothing on me. Nothing."

"Constable York, must you handcuff him? My word, he's not going to run off on you."

"Just rules. And we just got these new cuffs, want to try them out."

Thaddeus grinned. "I don't mind."

"Well, I mind!"

"Sorry, ma'am."

"Mr. York, how can I see my husband?"

"He'll be in the Rockland jail. Visiting days are Wednesdays between ten and four."

"Rockland is fifteen miles across Silver Bay! I have no way to get there. Can you bring him to Ellsworth instead?"

"Rockland."

"That's too far for me."

"Then you'll just have to wait," York snapped.

"Why, Joshua there is no reason to speak to me like that!"

"Mildred, none of this be Joshua's fault. He's just doing his job."

"Mrs. Gale—Mildred—I didn't mean to shout, my apologies about that. Thaddeus is right, I'm just following orders. As I said, I don't like this any more than you do. Can only tell you the rules. Rockland, ten to four on Wednesdays. And look, everyone knows Leroy was no good. Off the record, I'm glad Leroy Jennings is gone, but that don't make murder right."

"My husband did not kill anyone! I will tell the world, I will!"

"No need to visit me in the slammer. Be home in no time. They got nothing on me. No body, no nothing."

"Best you not talk now, Thaddeus," urged Joshua. "Save it for the attorney."

"Don't need no lawyering. Got nothing on me."

"Glad to hear it," said York.

"Joshua, please, at least let me pack some things."

"'Course. But he won't be needing clothes."

"Is there soap in...in Rockland?" I could not stand to say jail, prison, or slammer.

"Best you pack some."

In minutes, I put together a small satchel of necessities and gathered some cookies and lemonade for the trip uptown.

After handing the treats to Constable York, the pale-faced young driver, tiny in his oversized black jacket and trousers, snapped the reins and the dark horse lurched into a noisy trot.

After horse and buggy passed her house in dusty drama, Min came running.

My sister-in-law hugged me tight. "My dear, dear Mildred. Your Thaddeus offing that fella makes the world a better place. Don't you worry none. Everything's going to be all right."

39

I woke so early it was still dark the following morning, Sunday, October 27th. Three months pregnant and no nausea. Felt right good. And then I remembered. Thaddeus was in jail. Arrested. For murder.

I rolled over and curled up under the covers, deciding to sleep just as long as my body could let me.

Noon! I had never slept that late in my whole life. Come to think of it, I had never, ever slept in a house alone before. How delicious such blessed, uninterrupted rest and solitude felt.

I dressed quickly into my nearest housecoat. And put Thaddeus going to jail out of my mind. The day was mine. Alone. Nobody watching how much or what I did.

"Hey, chickies!" I called on my way to the henhouse. "How many have you got for me today? I missed breakfast, am some hungry, you know."

I reached under the complaining hens and placed their warm eggs in my bleached white apron, one hand holding it up like a little hammock.

"Four. I will eat them all myself, I will."

The sound of lard spattering in the iron skillet filled the kitchen. Added the eggs, which sizzled sharply as they struck the pan, their rich smell mixing nicely with dark coffee. In minutes, I had settled myself, meal in hand, on top of the porch stairs. How strange that Thaddeus was not out in the harbor on such a day of flat seas and clear sky. Marvin, Irville, and Jon had not gone out, either.

"Mildred?"

"Todd!"

"Forgive me for being so intrusive. I was just coming by in my regular search for mushrooms. If there is anything I can do for you, anything at all, please let me know."

"Thank you, Todd. I just cannot think of a thing. I am fine, I think."

"You do look fine. I mean, beg your pardon, well rested. Like you have been able to sleep amid all this...how to say it...island hoopla."

"I slept well last night. I only just woke up."

"So very late!"

"I have never slept so long or late in all my days. I do not know how I managed to, but the rest did me good."

"You must have needed it."

"Todd?"

"Yes?"

"I just thought of something you could do, maybe."

"Yes?"

"I am afraid it is a lot to ask."

"I doubt that."

"Well, we sure need a bookshelf at the school."

"I'd be glad to."

"Wonderful! I will try to get the director to reimburse you for the materials but am sure he will not go for labor."

"Don't worry about the materials. I've some decent eastern pine not going to any use."

"The children and I would be much obliged."

"I am so thrilled to help out. Count on me for the shelves."

"Thank you, Todd."

"You are a kind woman, Mildred. Everything you are going

through, yet you are still thinking of the children. Mind you, I am not surprised."

"Hale Harbor children deserve the best."

"They do. I hope I can maintain that standard with my woodworking." Todd's eyes squinted, and he took a step toward me. "Are you truly all right?"

"Yes, yes, I am fine, really."

He nodded. And touched my shoulder ever so slightly.

"Well, I have a job in town for the Chestertons, am biking up there later today. I am staying in their guesthouse while working, and then back here Thursday. May I come by the school on Friday for measurements?"

Let me come with you to the Chestertons'! I wanted to yell out loud.

"Friday is fine. And thank you for passing by."

"My pleasure."

Todd tipped his brown wool cap. With long strides, he walked across the lawn and toward the woods he foraged. Todd would not have walked across our lawn like that if Thaddeus had been home.

"Wait, Todd?"

"Yes?"

"Would you deliver a letter to the post office for me?"

"Certainly. I will come by on my way uptown."

"Thank you kindly."

"See you in a few hours."

I wolfed down my breakfast and ran inside. I would write a letter to Ma and send her the old one, too!

October 27, 1912

Dear Ma,

Need to hurry. Todd, a neighbor, is dropping by soon on his way to uptown Popplestone. He is going to send my mail.

I am pregnant! Please come visit as soon as you can. Bring Julia. I was nauseous for wee bit there in the beginning but feel mighty fine now.

I cannot wait to be a mama, and I am nervous, too. Thaddeus will be a good papa, I think. He works hard and well. Pa was right, Thaddeus Gale is a very good fisherman. Schooner captains come for his lobsters. Sometimes rusticators, too, from uptown. And lobster smacks.

Oh my, I am rushing this note. There is much to do today and yet I want to tell you everything at once.

I love my schoolhouse. The little building is about as big as the Perrys' shed and is a five-minute walk past Min's place (Ma, you must read this letter after my first, so you know about the people I mention). Thaddeus says he wants ten children, my! We will start with one. With only 17 (and a quarter) in the harbor now, we really need more. If you know of any families on Crescent that could buy or rent land, they are very welcome here. I am sure Todd could be hired to help build their house. And there is plenty of work to be had, especially if a man wants to fish (or woman, really, two women fished here before!). If they have school-age children, they will be especially welcome. Or young couples likely to have children. My, how lovely it would be to have some Crescent children in my school!

There is too much to say. Oh dear, I just do not have all the time or enough paper to tell you about my life. How is yours?

Goodbye for now, my beautiful Ma. I miss you so very much. Please give Pa, Julia, and the boys many big hugs from me.

Love, Mildred May

I carefully folded the note, crying for how deeply I missed everyone, and put it with the previous letter in a new envelope. I then sealed the envelope with glue and took two pennies for the stamp from a small tin box in the kitchen cupboard.

When Todd picked up the letter on his way to town, he insisted I not pay him for the stamp. I would rather accept charity than have Thaddeus know I sent the letters, so I accepted Todd's gift with only the tiniest bit of guilt.

And then, for the first time, I walked the western shore to Grouse Point. What a view to behold! Rocky coast and glittering ocean as far as the eye could see. My oh my, I lived in the most beautiful place in the world.

40

"**B**oys and girl!"

   Eager, obedient faces looked up from their studies.

"Mr. Calderwood will be here soon to consider where our new bookshelf will go. Please be on your best behavior for our guest."

"Aren't we being good now?" asked Orris.

"Indeed, you all are. Keep it up."

"Yes, ma'am."

Todd appeared at the large window next to the doorway moments later. He wore a blue-and-white checkered shirt neatly tucked into navy trousers. He wiped his feet on the outside mat and took off a blue cap. The man had a lot of caps. He paused, standing on the entry stairs, a doe and her fawn watching from the woods.

Eight little eyes riveted on our guest as if he were from outer space. Lucy tittered, and then cupped her hand over her mouth to stop.

"Mr. Calderwood, we are happily expecting you," I greeted.

"Good morning to you all."

"Good morning, Mr. Calderwood."

"Good morning, Mr. Calderwood."

"Good morning, Mr. Calderwood."

"Good morning, Mr. Calderwood."

"Students. You keep working on your writing while Mr. Calderwood and I talk about new shelves."

"Yes, ma'am."

"Yes, ma'am."

"Yes, ma'am."

"Yes, ma'am."

"Mr. Calderwood, let me show you where we would like the bookshelf."

Todd followed me a few paces across the room. The four students studied at their desks on the east side of the room, providing plenty of space for furniture along the western wall. Dozens of used books donated by summer rusticators were stacked on the six unused desks in the opposite corner, including a special one about astronomy for Orris. The books had appeared at the doorstep in four wooden crates one sunny Sunday morning after the start of the school year.

Todd whispered, "How are you doing, Mildred May?"

"Well enough."

"Have you heard anything from Rockland?"

"Not yet."

"Everything will be okay."

"I hope so."

"I think so."

"Thank you."

"In the meantime, and always, count on me."

"Thank you, Todd. Your support means a lot."

Todd then spoke in normal tones. "How high would you like them, Mrs. Gale?"

"Well, I do not rightly know. What do you suggest?"

"I would want them nearly the entire length of the wall, with the top within reach of your smallest anticipated student—your daughter or son in about five years."

"That sounds very good!"

"The top will be a nice spot to put anything you or the children like, such as art projects, items they collect, flowers, decorations. The bookshelves will be low for you, but for the youngsters, about right."

"For a single fellow, you are certainly in tune with children's needs."

"I am blessed with many nieces and nephews."

"How many?"

"Fourteen of them."

"My goodness! Where are they all?"

"Eastport, mostly. A few others are scattered about Maine, three in Boston, I believe."

"Might some of them visit you here on the island? We would love to have the children join us at school for a few days. If your house is too small, the families could stay with us, and I am sure Min would welcome house guests, also. We all would!"

Four heads swiveled our way, eyes wide and gleaming.

"Yes, please bring them Mr. Calderwood!" Lucy called.

Todd blushed and lowered his voice as he glanced at the hopeful children. "Regrettably, I don't see them now, since...well, I am a little bit distant from my older sister and younger brothers and parents these days, sadly...most regrettably. And several of their children are already adults, with children of their own already, I understand."

"Are all of your siblings also parents?"

"Yes, all six are parents, two are grandparents, that I know of."

"I am so very sorry you do not see them," I whispered.

"I am sorry, too, but never mind that. I am thrilled to help the children here, kind of makes up for not seeing the little ones in my family. I used to be the doting uncle, a role I cherished. Now I can be one again maybe, in a small way."

"Most certainly. You are an uncle to every Hale child."

"Well then, let me take some measurements. I'll have it done in a couple of weeks, how is that?"

"That fast? How fine!"

Todd bent down, pulled out his well-worn wooden ruler, unfolded it to full length, and extended it along the floor. He took out a tiny brown frayed notebook and wrote some numbers alongside a neatly sketched diagram.

Too quickly, he finished.

"Just as I thought. Bookshelves the length of the wall are just under the length of my boards. I have all the materials we need. I'll be going now, Mrs. Gale."

"Thank you ever so kindly, Mr. Calderwood."

The visitor flashed a broad smile that showed deeply experienced lines—and very good teeth.

"Goodbye, children. Study well and do yourselves proud."

The children smiled back, and then chimed in, led by Lucy:

"Goodbye, Uncle Calderwood!"

"Goodbye, Uncle Calderwood!"

"Goodbye, Uncle Calderwood!"

"Goodbye, Uncle Calderwood!"

Wearing an Orris-like wide grin, and carefully closing the door behind him so it would not slam, Todd left the school.

"You sweet on him?" Irville blurted out as soon as the visitor had walked down the stairs.

The other children and I looked at Irville in horrified fashion.

I felt myself blushing, maddeningly so. "Why Irville, whatever are you saying?"

"You seem sweet on him."

"Well, he is a very nice man, but I am not sweet on him, the way you mean. Young man, I am married."

"Don't stop some, you know."

Lucy frowned, and gave Irville a positively daggered look.

"Irville, what has gotten into you? That is an entirely inappropriate and impolite thing to say—or even to think!"

"I am sorry, ma'am." Irville hung his head, not hiding an impudent grin.

"If I were a different sort of teacher, you would be whipped for that kind of talk. I should put you in the corner."

Irville lost his smirk and looked up. "I am truly sorry, Teacher Gale."

"Apologies accepted. Let's get back to our studies. Irville, you will have more writing than the others for that outburst."

"Yes, ma'am."

As I watched the students and wondered how Irville had so

easily flustered me, I noticed a single teardrop slide down Samuel's face and land on his desk, darkening the wood in a tiny circle below his bowed head. The boy was writing so furiously his pencil tore up his notebook. I wanted to hug my Samuel but knew that would only make things worse for him.

Fifteen minutes later, Todd was back.

"Mrs. Gale?"

"Yes, Mr. Calderwood?"

"I almost forgot to give you your mail."

"My oh my, thank you!"

I took the precious package with two hands, a bundle of letters neatly stacked and bound with twine, admiring my name and address in Ma's handwriting. I raised the packet and smelled the letters, and then, embarrassed, swiftly tossed them onto my desk.

Todd said quietly, "I will check the post for you whenever I am uptown."

"Most grateful."

I wanted to hold Todd's hand, if only briefly, since I could not have my ma's.

"Ain't it time for astronomy studies?"

"*Isn't* it time for astronomy studies. You know better than to say *ain't*, Orris!"

"Yes, ma'am, I meant isn't, just slipped up there. Jon says ain't. My ma don't."

"Doesn't."

"Doesn't."

"Okay, my Orris. Let us go learn about the stars—and how to reach them, too."

"What? Go to the stars?"

"Why, yes. Every child can reach for the stars in life. Remember that, young man. Maybe someone will go to the moon and back. Maybe you someday."

"Me?" he replied, following his schoolmates inside. "You are in a mighty lofty mood, Teacher Gale."

"Why, Orris, good for you. What an excellent use of a fine word—*lofty*. Where did you learn it?"

"My mama used it."

"Good for her. Smart woman, your mother."

"She said my pa is in a lofty place, forever."

"Lofty place?"

"I think she meant heaven."

"I see. Are you sure that is what she meant?"

Orris smiled, standing tall, chest out. "She was sure. No more hitting us, not ever, she promised."

Todd and I stared at Orris. The boy *was* sure. The certainty of it played in his eyes. And he was happy. Genuinely happy, even for knowing what heaven meant to the living.

"You are positive your pop is not coming back?"

"Positive."

"Why so positive?"

"Because he is gone. Don't-ever-come-back kind of gone. That's what I heard Mr. Gale and Ma talk about. Mama and me are safe now."

41

I was walking home after that school day made particularly pleasant with Todd's visits and Ma's mail when Min ran toward me.

"Your Thaddeus! They've let him out already! He's arriving any time!"

My stomach turned wretched for reasons I could not figure. Yet this surely was good news. If Thaddeus was innocent, I could hold my head high. Innocent meant for a better papa, too.

Innocent, though, meant back to forever. My holiday in my home, over.

Back to cleaning and cooking and laundry and readying baths.

"Mildred, did you hear what I said?"

"How can he be back so fast? How do you know?"

Min explained, breathlessly, arms gesturing about, "Bud Beverage told me uptown. Came around by sail. Said he saw Thaddeus and the warden loading up over there in Rockland earlier today. Fish warden bringing him home. 'They've nothing on him,' said Bud!"

"Nothing on him, innocent."

"Got out fast. Not even a week. Good sign."

"Best I get home and make a welcome meal."

"That you should. Poor man. Been through hell and back, I expect."

"No good being accused for nothing."

"Ain't that the truth."

I walked a little brisker, a little lighter, a little prouder. I straightened the boots on the porch and went inside. I stood in the doorway trying to figure out what to do first, watching my dresses flap on the clothesline near horizontally. Such a blustery day to venture between islands. Maybe the fish warden would decide not to make the crossing? I went inside to a dirty, cluttered-up house. Thaddeus had been gone less than a week. How could such messiness happen so fast?

"Well, no use standing around," I said to nobody.

Reading Ma's letters would have to wait.

I started with the dishes, using cold water. Then I washed the cherry-wood countertops and swept the floor. Oh my, the bed! I ran upstairs and made it for the first time since Thaddeus had gone. Clothes on the floor! I dropped them in the laundry basket. What to cook? When would he be home? The windows looked smudgy!

"MILDRED! I'M HOME."

The voice bellowing from outside was so rough I nearly tripped on a shirt clumped on the floor. I yanked it up and threw it in with the rest of Thaddeus's clothes. *Should have done his washing before mine*, I thought much too late.

I ran back downstairs.

"Thaddeus!" I wrapped my arms around his big frame as he came in the door.

He embraced me, quickly bringing his hand to my bottom. Too fast.

"You must be hungry."

"I am. Not for food," his voice gruff, demanding, not asking.

I let him take my hand and lead me upstairs. I had not seen him in a week, after all, seemed I should want to.

"You must be tired," I pleaded. He sat on the bed, lifting his legs to remove his long black socks.

"Nope. Not me," replied Thaddeus. "Get undressed."

"Just like that?"

"Just like that."

And he did it, just like that. In a way I could not understand.

The next morning, I held our thick bedcovers up to my neck as I watched him dress. He seemed downright ugly to me for the first time with that big, bulky, over-muscled body, craggy face, and thinning hair covering baldness I had not noticed previously. Would our child inherit such a large hooked nose?

I was some relieved when he snapped his suspenders in place. And then felt wretched again as he said, "Been wanting to do that to a woman all week. Goddamn prison! Bunch of hooligans in there thinking they can do anything they want to you. Well, they didn't. They got it where they tried to give it! I am always the stronger man. Don't nobody can never forget it."

I leaned over the bed and threw up in the basket of dirty clothes.

42

"Mildred, dear, brought you breakfast."

Thaddeus stood by the bed, wearing a fresh shirt he had found somewhere, holding a tray of runny fried eggs, toast and apple butter, even coffee.

"Cat got your tongue?" Thaddeus winked as he spoke.

"Did not expect breakfast," I managed curtly.

"Hope this makes up for...um, that... Don't know what got into me last night."

"Doesn't."

"I love you, you know. Have a funny way of showing it sometimes."

"It was horrible!"

"I know. Damn jail that was, not my fault!"

"Of course it was your fault!"

"Trying to say I'm sorry! What else do you want?"

"Not this!"

Thaddeus placed the tray on the bed. His hands shook.

"Have breakfast. Going fishing. You rest up. Must have been a long week with me gone."

Thaddeus leaned in to kiss me on the cheek. I flinched. He stopped short.

"I understand." He touched my shoulder and left.

After hearing the front door close, I sat up and pulled the tray toward me so fast some coffee slopped onto the tray. I jabbed at the eggs, causing the yolks to further run across the plate. Piling them onto bread with my knife, I took soggy bites, stuffing them into my mouth with two hands.

Nobody had ever served me breakfast in bed before.

Breakfast and more sleep fortified me, though a heavy weight still clamped onto my heart. Returning to overdue housework, I started with my plate caked with dried egg yolk. Thank goodness for Saturday and no school. And with how many days he had missed at sea, Thaddeus would stay away late. In five hours, I cleaned the entire house and did the laundry, including washing out my own vomit, eliminating every last speck of my holiday.

I pulled out my satchel bulging with art homework. I wanted to get schoolwork done before rewarding myself with Ma's letters.

Lucy, that dear girl! Her drawing showed a young dancing princess in a blue gown flying above the Bell Farm peninsula. That child deserved an art teacher.

I chuckled at Orris's work. He drew a scribbly, stick-figured boy by the harbor looking up at a very accurately drawn Big Dipper.

Sam's artwork showed his father standing tall in a peapod just inside the harbor by the ledge, bravely reaching with extra-long arms for a giant lobster lurching at him from atop a cresting wave.

Irville drew himself, thick dark hair blowing in the breeze, holding a spear and poised to strike a great silver swordfish.

I spoke out loud. "That's it! Each student could have one frame, and the top of those Calderwood bookshelves will be covered with their ongoing, rotating artwork."

I wished Todd would drop by the house again but knew he would steer a wide path with Thaddeus home.

"Pish-tosh!" I admonished myself for such thoughts.

And then thought them again.

Finally, time for Ma's letters! I pulled the mail out of my bag and yanked the twine tied in a bow. Six letters slid out of the bundle. To my delight, I noticed two were from Julia. I would start with the oldest one: July 1, 1912, nearly five months previous.

I devoured each note, thinking between each delicate page how lucky I was to have Todd as my private mailman.

My ma and everyone in the family were doing just fine! Well, Foster broke his arm falling out of a tree, but was healing fast and well. Nobody sick, not even a cold. And even though she had not yet heard of my baby coming, Ma was planning to visit in the spring-time with Julia. Julia was sorry she did not say goodbye to me at the beach, had been too torn up about me leaving, but was doing better. In her own hand and with heart drawings, she told me how much she loved me.

Relishing the sweet distraction of news from home, I put Thaddeus's ogre-like behavior out of my head until supper.

Candles flickered light across Thaddeus's weathered face as we sat at our tiny table. Only thirty-five, Thaddeus's deep lines from time on the water made him look older than Todd. Confronting Thaddeus was not something I wanted to do, but it was something I had to do, could feel that coming on strong—was the Combs in me.

The harbor ran dark and slow that evening.

I slammed the pot of soup in the middle of the table. "So, what happened to Leroy?"

"None of your business!"

"When my husband is arrested, is my business."

"No it ain't!"

"You better not have killed that fellow."

"So what if I did?"

"I would not like you much then."

"Everyone else in the harbor likes the idea of me offing him. Am a hero over it. Why can't you be like the other women and worship me?"

"Worship you?"

"Why not?"

"I do not worship you. I do not think anyone else is worshiping you, either."

"Maybe I mean more to this here harbor than I mean to you."

"Thaddeus!"

"What?"

"Did you, or did you not, kill Leroy?"

"What do you think?"

"I hear things."

"Hear things? You going crazy on me?"

"No, not like that. At school."

"What them kids say?"

"Do not call them kids. They are *children*."

"What them children say?"

"Orris said Leroy is not coming back, not ever."

Thaddeus sipped his vegetable soup quieter than usual. He put the bowl on the table with a *thunk*. "So?"

"Sounded like he knew Leroy was dead or something."

"So?"

"So? Well, he—Orris, that is—Orris said you and Pearl talked about Leroy never coming back, that he was in a 'lofty place,' like heaven."

Thaddeus let out a hard laugh, knocking his knees on the bottom of the table. Soup bowl tottered, half of it spilling out.

"Well, my goodness!" I exclaimed mopping up tiny chunks of potato dropping to the floor as the carrot-orange broth oozed off the side of the table. "How might *that* be so funny?"

"Leroy wouldn't never make it past the pearly gates to heaven."

"You know what I mean. I have to ask."

"No, you don't."

"I do."

Thaddeus let out a sigh, "Young boys have active imaginations, Mildred. Surprised you got suckered in."

"I know about children's imaginations, but it was so disturbing, I mean—" I coughed and looked down, away from Thaddeus. "Sounded like...like..."

"I killed him."

I looked up. "You killed him?"

"No. Was just finishing your sentence, like."

"But you said, 'I killed him.'"

"To finish your sentence. Not *because* I killed him!"

"Well, what did Orris mean when he said 'don't-come-back-kind of gone'?"

"You just don't quit, do you?"

"Not usually."

"Mildred May! Leroy would've killed that woman and boy sooner or later. Which be worse—him or them?"

"What are you saying?"

"Nothing. Just good he's gone. Wish I'd killed my father."

"What?"

"Said I wish I *had* killed Leroy."

"You said you wish you had killed your father."

"I did?"

"You did."

"Well, there's that, too. Wish I had."

"Killed your father?"

"Not talking about that now!"

"You brought it up."

"I'm ending it, too. Don't ask me about it."

"Thaddeus!"

"What?"

"Did Jon kill his father?"

"Mildred—"

"I am your wife. I have to know!"

"Okay, okay. Set yourself down, calm yourself down, and I'll tell you."

43

I sat, with my husband, at our table.

"I am listening."

"Okay, Mildred, here's the damn straight truth of it. Big Leroy went after Pearl the night of your lobster chowder party. She had cooked him and Jon supper late that evening and Leroy didn't like it—damn stupid reason to hit a gal! Still blind drunk that son of a bitch Leroy was, was about to punch her when Jon whacked him on the head with a skillet. When I met up with him in the harbor, Jon blubbered up his confession: 'I thought he'd just be knocked out!' the boy said. Jon whacked Leroy harder than he meant to, I guess. Was an accident. He was protecting Pearl."

"Jon would have never gone to jail for that."

"Jon and Pearl didn't know nothing, were scared of the law. Dragged Leroy to the shed for the night and then into the boat right early the next morning. Jon rowed out over a mile, laid big old Leroy up with nets and rocks, and just let him go. After messing with the body like that and being helped by Pearl, he couldn't very well report anything to York, now, could he?"

"No, I suppose not. Jon is young. He did not know what to do, and neither did Pearl. Too bad, that, we all would have helped them.

Constable York would have understood, too. Self-defense clear as can be."

"Yes, we all would have, but once that body be gone, was too late. So I helped."

"That morning you thought Jon was poaching and went out there after him. I saw you talking, and then shaking hands. You made a deal?"

"Yes. And that deal didn't include you knowing a dang thing!"

"I am your wife. I see and hear things."

"Learning that."

"You pretended you killed a man because it made you even more of a legend around here. That is what you want, to be the big hero in the harbor?"

"Is being a hero so bad? Saved Jon, too, remember."

"Saving Jon is a good thing. The bravado, not good, is a lie."

"Damn it, Mildred! I took credit for offing Leroy because it's more believable *I'd* do something like that, for us all! And there was no body, so no conviction. Took the chance. Did it for my harbor."

"Always for the harbor, not for me. What about our child? He will grow up thinking his father killed a man!"

"Good!"

"Not good! Not even the truth! And what about Orris?"

"Orris was sleeping, didn't see a thing. He don't know nothing. Little boy like that shouldn't have to see a brother kill his pa, or even know about it."

Thaddeus's voice cracked as he spoke of Orris. I thought he was going to cry. I reached for his hand across the table then. He let me take it.

As he caressed the back of my hand, Thaddeus continued, "Mildred, don't go yapping to any uptowners coming down here about me telling that dog Leroy I'd kill him if he went after my traps. Far as I know, nobody from Hale squawked about that night. Don't need no second investigation. Is just fine harbor folk think I done him in out on the water over poaching—that be a good enough reason to kill someone—but best not let that get around the whole dang island."

"I won't, Thaddeus. Anyway, you did not kill him, I am happy for that."

"Don't say nothing about Jon, neither. That boy gets arrested, well then with no one to support them out here, Pearl and Orris will have to leave too, and who knows what would become of them. Another family, gone. Your student, gone."

"I will not tell a soul."

"That's my girl now. You know, Mildred, Jon is a good fisherman, taking him under my wing, I am. They'll be fine. Sixteen is plum old enough to support a family."

"Yes, I suppose it is out here. But I still do not like everyone thinking you are a murderer."

"How about hero—you like them thinking that?"

"Again, no, not when it is a lie."

"Nothing we can do about all that, is for the good of the harbor."

"The harbor is more important to you than your own family!"

"Both be important. They be intertwined. See there, I know some big words too, teacher."

"Stop making fun of me."

"I am not. I...Mildred, truly, I do love you. You should hear that more often. Am sorry again about last night. Don't think it'll happen again."

I dropped his hand then, remembering, and we spoke no more that evening. *Don't think it'll happen again* was not good enough for me.

44

On the following Monday morning, Todd showed up before recess to check a couple of measurements.

We sat on the steps, watching the children skitter along the road rolling hoops.

"You have been on my mind," he said.

"And you on mine. I am so glad you are here. I have no one I can really talk to."

"What about the women?"

"They talk amongst each other."

"You cannot trust them—to be private, that is? Not even Mineola?"

"Especially Min. Her husband is Thaddeus's brother!"

"I see. And what of Thaddeus?"

"Thaddeus?"

"You and he talk?"

"We talk, yes, but not like you and I do. Different subjects."

"Well, that would be natural, Mildred."

"I suppose so."

"You can trust me. You know I would never share, nor judge. Is something bothering you?"

I stared at a distant point while thinking about Thaddeus's first night home from Rockland, how he was in bed, and how he was lying to everyone about who really killed Leroy.

"Mildred?"

"I apologize. Seems my mind is drifting."

"You have a lot to do. I should go." He started to get up.

"No!"

He sat down abruptly. "Okay, I'll stay."

"I mean, I am fine. Thaddeus is fine. It is good he is home, all happened so suddenly, is all."

Todd frowned. "Are you all right, Mildred May? It should be absolutely splendid a husband is home."

I fought tears. We were at school. I could not cry.

I felt Todd's hand on my arm. "Everything will be okay."

I let out the breath I did not know I was holding. "Thank you, Todd. You are such a friend. And I need your help."

"Anything."

"There is a rumor going around that Thaddeus really did kill Leroy, have you heard it?"

Todd looked at his shoes. "I have heard it."

"Do you believe it?"

He waited a long time before answering.

"I don't know what to believe, Mildred. All I know, for sure, is that you are a good woman. If Thaddeus killed Leroy, it has nothing to do with you and who you are. If he did not kill him, well then, so much the better."

"Todd, I promised Thaddeus I would not tell a soul, but I cannot keep this inside. I need your help keeping a rather big secret."

"I will keep your secret, I promise."

"Jon killed Leroy."

"Not Thaddeus, really?"

"You don't believe me?"

"Well, it's just that...the fight at your house and all...Thaddeus seems the logical one. Just can't imagine Jon being able to stand up to such a big man...his own father...and well, everyone assumes Thaddeus took care of the situation."

"My husband did not kill Leroy!" I fairly shouted.

"I believe you!" Todd glanced toward the faraway children and then took my hand. "So sorry to offend."

"I am sure Jon did it, in self-defense."

"Poor Jon, he is just a boy, really. What happened?"

I told him everything Thaddeus had said to me about Leroy's death.

He responded firmly. "Jon was only protecting Pearl. The law would have protected Jon. We would have all helped him."

"That is exactly what I told Thaddeus! He said it was too late, was up to him to save Jon, and now everyone thinks my husband is a murderer."

"That bothers you."

"Of course it bothers me."

"I suggest you let it go, Mildred. This place—well...not only in this harbor...in Gooseneck, uptown Popplestone, and Preacher Cove, too—I don't know, sometimes people just let bad things go. Over in Gooseneck especially, someone like Leroy Jennings would just keep beating his wife until she died or managed to run off. Murder's not right, but neither is wife beating."

"It was still wrong to get rid of the body like that. The man deserved a decent burial."

"Leroy Jennings was a man of the sea."

"That is not funny!"

"I didn't mean it as a joke. Mildred, you know as well as I an island takes care of its own, sometimes for better, sometimes for worse."

"That sounds like marriage vows."

"In many ways, living on a small island is like making a marriage vow, I would imagine."

"But I cannot stand people, especially children, thinking Thaddeus is a murderer!"

"Then do not think about it."

"Are your solutions always so simple?"

"Probably. Comes from most things being too complicated for me to endure, so I simplify them."

"I am sorry to hear that, Todd."

"Me too. Will probably tell you about it someday, but not today, and not here."

"I am here when you need me."

"I know you are, Mildred, thank you."

"I wish letting it go was that simple. Not worrying is difficult for me."

"I know, and I am sorry."

"How did you change?"

"Had to. The worrying got too much."

"Again, you make it sound so simple."

"Wasn't simple. Just took time. And perspective."

"Time and perspective. All right, maybe I can wait for those."

45

Sunny days continued that November, not tricking us islanders knowing winter was coming in its determined way. Irville Senior, Marvin, and Jon met Thaddeus every morning on the Gale stone wharf no matter the weather, fair or foul. Thaddeus arrived last, just after his boys set up the tandem boats with gear.

If skies too dark or seas too rough, Thaddeus called off the day or limited fishing to inside the harbor. I was some proud he took proper care of his working fellas by not taking chances out there.

I took Todd's advice and let things go. Everyone seemed to forget about Leroy's disappearance anyway. They were too busy getting on with their lives. I had to get on with mine.

Once a week, the five-masted schooner *Dorothy Jean* anchored in the harbor, her captain buying Bell Farm produce by the bushel. On rare calm days, Wabanaki Indians, most of the Penobscot Nation, paddled in for goods and to sell sweetgrass baskets, their birch canoes looking tiny next to some of the largest vessels sailing the Gulf of Maine. I hoped to see one of Maine's ten six-masted schooners, but none arrived that first year.

Aside from the day at school when he delivered the new bookshelf and everybody cheered, I only saw Todd in the distance. Families kept to themselves, shoring up houses, canning vegetables, harvesting wood, and cleaning up outside in preparation for winter.

Thaddeus stayed away from me in bed, guilty for how he had treated me after his time in prison. I was grateful for the distance.

When not teaching, I cleaned house and did the chores. I rearranged furniture in the extra bedroom, thinking of Ma and Julia sleeping there in the spring. And there was the small back bedroom, the baby's room, to do something about. The room was empty, not even a crib.

In the middle of an afternoon cleaning, I heard another *Bang! Bang! Bang!* on the door.

I was relieved not to see Constable York. "Eve, come in. Have a seat. And a snack."

"Oh, Mildred, how could you? My waist just don't need this."

She helped herself to the plumpest donut on the plate.

"Your waist is just fine."

"And yours. Mildred, you are a stunning pregnant woman."

"Why thank you, but I...I am a little worried, feel right strange in there."

"Well then, that's why I came by, to see how you were doing with the baby. 'Course you feel strange. Have a little human growing inside. No matter how many people say how natural it is, is just plain queer-like to be growing a baby. Giving birth is even stranger!"

"It does feel queer. Feels like, well, something is fluttering. What is that?"

"Feels like a butterfly?"

"Why yes, it does!"

Eve smiled wide.

"That, my dear Mildred, is your baby. Is little, is all, feels like a wispy fluttering butterfly when it swims about. And he, or she, is fine. Didn't your mother ever tell you about that when she was having your brothers?"

"No, she didn't. I thought something was wrong."

"Not wrong. All *right*. Still, when are you going to see Doc Hornby? It's about time to check on things."

"I really do not know when I can see a doctor so far away. I wish I knew when the baby is due though."

"I can tell you that right now."

"Yes, please!"

"When did you first miss your cycle?"

"Ahh, well, that would be around the last half of August."

"Can't be any closer than that?"

"Not really."

"Well then, your little boy or girl is due within May, simple as that."

"I am only just three months pregnant? May seems a long way away."

"Not long, you'll see. Time is going to start speeding up on you, always does. And you sure don't want to give birth in the winter."

"True about winter babies, and I hope you are right about time passing quickly."

"Mildred, could your mother visit when all the men leave for their last hurrah fall fishing, before winter? She'd be nice company, could keep an eye on you, too, and help around the house while you teach."

"She and my sister plan to visit in the spring. Last hurrah?"

"Two miles out."

"Two miles out?"

"You don't know. Thaddeus, Irville, Marvin, and I suppose Jon now, too, follow the lobsters to deeper water with a few traps they haul over and over again. Don't make any sense for them to come back daily after rowing so far, so they camp out on outer islands and fish and whatever else for two or three weeks."

"Outer islands? You mean farther than those we can see from here? I thought there was nothing out there."

"Way, way out there are a couple small, uncharted islands smack-dab in the middle of nowhere on the eastern side. Might be the only islands between here and England, for all we know. Boys call them Hell and Hell Again."

"My word! Nobody on Crescent Island does that kind of fishing."

"Makes us all nervous as all heck. One storm on their way out or back, and more than half the men of the harbor, all of the fisher-men...gone."

"Thaddeus did not say a thing about this."

"Suppose he did not want to worry you, baby and all."

"I suppose."

Later that evening, I yelled at Thaddeus the moment he walked in. "You never tell me anything!"

"Can't I have my bath first? Is some cold out there, I tell you. What I do now?"

"Hell and Hell Again?"

"Told Marvin and Irville to tell Min and Eve to say nothing about that."

"Eve told me."

"Can't keep a secret, that one."

"Why the secret? I would have found out soon enough."

"You would."

"Why then?"

"Didn't want to worry you none."

"Thing is, Thaddeus, when you keep secrets like this, I wonder what else you are lying about."

"Not lying, just not telling."

"Is the same to me."

"I'll try to do better, still learning marrying ways, how's that?"

"Promising is better than saying you will try."

"I promise to try my best, how'd that be?"

"A bit better."

"All right then, better it is."

46

The worst happened Saturday afternoon, November 16th.

That morning I busied myself preparing Thaddeus and the other three fishermen to bed down on the frigid islands of Hell or Hell Again, packing layers of woolen clothes, heavy blankets, piles of bread, smoked fish, and dried deer meat. They left at midday with lunches to eat along the way, Thaddeus and Irville rowing, Jon and Marvin in the sterns, gear set evenly between the boats and towing another for their expected haul of deep-water lobsters.

Pearl and Orris, Eve and her sons, Min and I waved to our fellas until they turned into tiny dots and rounded the harbor corner where we could see them no more.

"Tea at my house, ladies!" Min announced.

"You all go," I said. "I am not feeling so fine."

"You sick?"

"No, tired is all."

"Go on and rest, then. Eve? Pearl?"

"Need to make lunch for the boys," said Eve.

"Me too, for Orris," said Pearl. "I'm sorry, Min."

"Lunch for all the boys and their moms, too, then, my house, not taking no for an answer."

"Hooray!" Sam cried, jumping into the air. "Auntie Min's venison stew, I bet."

"Venison stew it is. Made a batch for the big boys' supper tonight. Saved plenty for the young ones."

Three women and three boys headed up the road to Min's place.

I trudged inside and lay down on our bed, despondent over news from home. I had found the letter on my school desk the day before. Although she and Pa and Julia and the boys were thrilled with my pregnancy, Ma would not come visit when the baby came. She had too much to do on Crescent.

Something wet and clammy warmed my thighs. Did my bladder let go? No. Blood. Lots of blood!

Groaning, I put my hand to my stomach hoping for it to hurt. I wanted it to hurt! But it would not hurt even a little bit.

I should have expected a miscarriage but had not thought about it once.

And I should have seen Doc Hornby like Eve told me to.

My baby was dead. Gone! Like she never was. I felt too hollow to even cry out. I was so tired. I wanted to wail. I did not. *Clean up!* screamed my head. If nobody saw, or knew, then maybe it did not happen!

No baby for the harbor.

But she was *my* loss!

Something moved in my throat, digging in with dull talons.

Clean. I must clean! The bed soaked in it! In her! I had to hurry! Before that stain set! I pulled up the sheet and yanked off the mattress pad. Clean. Had to clean.

I bundled up everything in my arms. Feeling weak and unsteady, I rushed downstairs.

Failed my child.

Failed my husband.

Failed myself.

Failed my neighbors.

Failed Hale Harbor.

I dumped the sheet and pad into the empty bathtub in the living room and went to the kitchen to get water to boil, raising and lowering the red lever of the well pump with all my strength. Must boil them, maybe they would get clean...oh please, get clean. Could not stand the sight of it!

More blood trickled down my leg.

As that lump clawed even harder along my throat, Todd walked up my porch stairs whistling a dandy tune, thumbs hooked in each of his front pockets.

I threw open the door, fell into his arms and let the lump turn into its most terrible wail.

"My dearest Mildred!"

He held me tightly and used his body to push me back into the kitchen. I felt his heart pounding and knew he was scared.

We stood like that for some time in the kitchen, my cries subsiding into short, hiccupping whimpers.

"Mildred, let's sit. What is going on? I am so sorry, and whatever it is, it will be okay."

I released my grip. We parted. His face grimaced as he looked at my red-soaked crotch through my blue-flowered dress, the one I had worn when Thaddeus had proposed. My blood was smeared on Todd's trousers.

"Mildred May, is the baby, isn't it. I am so sorry."

"Yes," barely a whisper.

"Please, sit, let me get you some warm water to drink."

He helped me ease into a wooden chair.

"Clothes. You need clothes. May I go to your bedroom?"

I nodded.

Todd put on a kettle and then ran upstairs, returning with my dark-green sweater dress and a pair of underwear.

"These all right?"

"Yes."

He went into the living room, closing the door behind him.

I changed, dropping the bloodied clothes on the floor and kicking them into a corner.

A knock. "May I come in now?"

"Yes."

Todd poured from the kettle and handed me a mug, wisps of

191

steam rising from its center. "It won't take me long to go to town on my bicycle. I heard a Boston doctor is visiting the island. I will find him."

"No!"

"No?"

"I do not want to see a doctor."

"But Mildred, you need to!"

"It is done. She's gone. I do not need a doctor to tell me that."

"I am so sorry."

"Todd, what if I cannot have children?"

"You can. This is only a first try."

"But my ma took thirteen years to have my sister Julia! And you know what? Min is in her tenth year of no baby and has given up. Flora had a problem when having Lucy, and there will be no more for her and Miles. What if I am the same? What if I cannot?"

"I really think you will," he said, taking my hands in his. "There's a reason this one did not...work out. It will be better next time, I can almost promise."

"Could you please hold me again, Todd? I cannot be alone with this."

Todd pulled up a chair and wrapped his arms around me.

We stayed embraced like that for a long time.

I would not have survived that day without him.

47

Todd and I spoke again inside my house that following Friday, after school. He had been checking on me every day for six days since I'd lost my baby. He took the side path and the back door so his visits were not for all in the harbor to see.

"Mildred, you must tell someone! The women. Mineola? You should tell one of the women."

"I know. I most definitely do not want to."

He took my hand. "Mildred, promise me, tell someone very soon, within two days."

I sighed. "I promise."

"Okay, good. I should go. This doesn't look right, me being here so often. Someone is going to notice eventually." He put on his sandy-brown cap.

"I do not care anymore about that."

"I know, but you will, if wrong things are said. This is my fault, for coming by. It is just that I...I...I think of you every time I wake up. I seem to have to see you. I am so worried about you."

"Kiss me," I heard myself say.

He looked as startled as I was with the plea.

"On the cheek. There is no harm in that."

"No harm in that." He took off his cap.

The man leaned to me then, and delicately kissed me on my left cheek. The lightest, sweetest touch I have ever known.

"Remember, Mildred May Gale, you made me a promise."

"I will keep it." I stood on my tiptoes and kissed him back. On the cheek.

Todd grinned, put his cap back on and walked out the back door.

He returned the next day, and the day after.

We sat at my little table overlooking the harbor.

"Have you kept your promise?" Todd sipped his coffee, watching me carefully.

"Not yet."

"You have until the end of today."

"A deadline?"

"A deadline. Why are you so hesitant?"

"I do not know. Maybe you are all I need."

"But they are women."

"Indeed."

"You don't think they care for you?"

"Not like you do."

"You still need to keep the promise. A miscarriage is not something one can keep secret for any length of time."

"I know. Later today, a promise."

We were quiet then, for an extended pause, and it was comfortable.

I kept my word. Mineola cried almost as much as I had the previous weekend. My only fib was the date, telling her it had happened a few days earlier, not a week before. I just could not tell anyone right away, I said, and that was the mighty truth within the lie.

I waited days, but except for Todd's daily visits, neighbors did not come around the house. Nobody offered baskets of bread and casseroles or to help with household chores. Nobody even came by with condolences.

48

The first day of December, fifteen days after losing my baby and a week after Min knew, I could stand it no longer.

That Sunday was so warm it practically begged me to get out of the house.

My first stop was Eve's.

"Is something to see you, Mildred," Eve called from the front porch. "I would expect you to be resting at home on a Sunday."

"I feel better now."

"Have a seat. Can you help me shell some peas? Still got some from my inside window garden."

"Certainly."

We sat on the Thomas porch overlooking field and harbor. I picked the ends off the pods and pushed the hard peas out with my thumb, dropping them into a small wooden bowl.

"Did Min tell you about my miscarriage?"

"Mildred! Do not say that word! We'll not talk about it no more!"

"So you know."

"'Course I know."

"And you did not even come by the house."

"No."

"Why not?"

"Bad luck."

"Bad luck?"

"Something like that, well, just forget about it and try again. Sooner Thaddeus gets home, the better for us all."

"Why, I cannot!"

"You must."

"*You* could have another!"

"Why are you so angry at me? Done my part. More than my part! Have two, the most any other woman has, by double, or triple, in the case of Min."

"You cannot multiply anything by zero and get anything but zero."

"What are you talking about?"

"Basic math."

"What?"

"Never mind. Why do you blame Min, the woman? What about the men? They have equal responsibility in all this."

"Humph, not how it works."

"I never heard of a woman having a baby without a man participating."

"You know what I mean."

"I do not. You have two, good for you and Irville. Others have one or none is fine, too."

"Not so fine around here, you should know that by now."

Eve fondled the top silver button on her swanky white sweater that looked like it had come from Europe, and I wondered if the rumors were true about her and that Smith fella. Had never seen her wear that sweater when Irville Senior was around.

She scooped up another pile of pea pods scattered on the weathered table, snapping off the tiny ends as she spoke. "Amazing we still got these snap peas. Surely the last of them, though."

I was glad for the change of subject. "They look good. Eve, I just thought of something!"

"What is that?"

"Look at these pea pods."

"So?"

"They are in the shape of a peapod—the boat."

"Well I'll be! Never thought about it that way."

"Neither have I. Surely, though, this is where the name came from."

"I won't look at any fisherman's peapod the same again."

"I hope they are doing all right out there on Hell islands."

"They should be. You know, Mildred, we owe your Thaddeus a big world of thanks."

"Why thank Thaddeus?"

"I mean, everyone figures. Big Leroy. The man didn't just up and leave."

"What else could he have done? He is not here."

"Nobody saw him leave."

"Whatever are you insinuating, Eve?"

"Why do you always use such big words?"

"I am a teacher. Using big words is my prerogative."

"Speak normal!"

"What exactly are you saying about Thaddeus?"

"Well..."

"Just spit it out!"

I threw the shell of a pea pod so hard it bounced off the table and hit Eve. She winced and touched her cheek.

She took a deep breath. "Okay, I'll say it! Mildred May Gale, we all think Thaddeus killed Leroy. And we are all mighty glad for it, too."

"My husband did not kill Leroy Jennings!"

"Stop being so angry!"

"No proof one way or the other."

"Well, what else happened? Leroy deserved it. Some stupid to poach like he did, was like he was possessed or something. Leroy was bad. Real bad. Pearl and Jon and Orris are better off without him. We all are."

"Ending a life is wrong, even that of a man who is doing bad things."

"We all think Leroy would have killed Pearl, and maybe even little Orris. Would that be right, to sit by and let him do that?"

"Well, no, but there is the law."

"What law would arrest someone because he *might* do something bad? Your Thaddeus stopped Big Bad Leroy in his tracks. The island way is the only way."

I stood up and yelled, "I meant it is against the law to murder someone! Murder is always wrong!"

Eve continued louder, throwing more peas into the bowl as she stood up.

"What Thaddeus did stopped murder of the worst kind, that of a sweet, unprotected woman and her child. Pre-happening, that's what I call it."

"You mean preemptive. Or premeditative."

"Whatever. You're the teacher."

We continued to throw peas at the bowl, some of them bouncing out and rolling off the table.

"Thaddeus did not kill Leroy. I just lost a child. You are saying if I have another, the child's father is a murderer."

"I'm not."

"That *is* what you are saying."

"I am saying your husband is a savior, not a killer. See there, you're not the only one to know big words."

"Thaddeus is no savior, any more than he is a killer!"

"You just set your mind on making a new harbor baby, that's what we need. What you need, too. Would calm you down some."

"I best be going now," I said curtly.

"Come by any time," she said just as sharply.

"I will," I lied as I turned and left.

Eve called to my back, "Don't wait long after he comes back to tell Thaddeus about it, if that's what you be thinking. The man has a right to know."

49

I went on my way to Pearl's and Flora's, suddenly veering left into the small wooded area partially hiding Todd's home.

He opened the door before I could knock. Todd looked right and left as I ducked under his arm and slipped in.

We sat, quiet, in two wooden chairs, close enough for me to smell his coffee'd breath, our fingers touching each other in tiny, gentle grasps.

"Good to see you, Mildred."

"I had to see you."

"Are you all right?"

"No. According to Eve, I am not to discuss my loss with anyone! Just forget about that baby, she said in so many words, focus on a new one. And hurry up and tell Thaddeus. Why, that woman cares more about my husband than my feelings, or even my health!"

"You need time to grieve!"

"Am I taking too long?"

"Certainly not. This harbor...some of the ideas...well, they are backward. There are such wonderful things about island life. Other things, not so good."

"Do you think Flora knows?"

"I really have no idea."

"I cannot imagine her being so cruel as not to come by. I do not need baskets of treats. I would like kind words, is all."

"I will always have kind words for you."

"I know, is one of the things I love about you." I wanted to kiss him then. On the lips. I did not.

"You know, Mildred, I so adore my nieces and nephews and have always wanted a child of my own. I envy you being able to do that, in as much time as you need, and you have plenty. Don't let island harbor pressure and petty gossip get to you."

"You are the one with plenty of time."

"I don't think I will ever have a child."

We fell silent then, our hands together.

We sat in quiet for a long time that afternoon, never letting go of each other. For a while, I rested my head on his shoulder. He did not move. We did not speak.

What I imagined was appalling. Yet I feared and hoped he imagined the same.

When I finally stood, he looked up at me and said, "I want to be good for you, Mildred, not cause you any trouble. I care for you too much to be anything else. Please, you must know that."

"You are good for me."

"I am here for you, as you need me, when you need me, the very second you need me. And I wish you could stay, but go you must. To avoid misunderstandings within the harbor."

"I am more comfortable here than in my own house."

"Is comfortable having you here."

Todd stood up then, peered out the window and nodded to me. Again I wanted to kiss him.

Again I did not.

I slipped out, hurried home, and got ready for the fishermen's return.

50

On a Saturday a week later, I spotted three dark specks well beyond the harbor as I hung freshly washed clothes inside, next to the stove. An hour later, the four men rowed in, their boats pushing plate-sized saucers of ice out of the way. Three boats rode deep in the gray water with men and traps, lobsters piled so high in the towed dory there would be crushed bugs on the bottom that would quickly become stew.

"Must be dang tired," said Min, who had appeared from the back of the house, bundled up and holding a steaming mug of coffee for Marvin. "Look at their shoulders, all slumped, they are."

"Right you are, Min. Three weeks away, they are going to appreciate proper beds and warm food."

"Been to hell and back!"

"Yes, indeed."

Min continued, "Our boys sure are smart following them lobsters out while the rest of the fishermen give up catching any closer to shore."

"Smart and hardworking."

"Got that right."

Before long, the tired men tied the boats up to the wharf, where

Pearl and Eve and their sons joined Min and me to help unload. The boys would fill the natural seawater pound with their catch, where they would stay and be fed in captivity with the last remaining herring until sold for a premium.

"Mildred, you go on home, dear," Min ordered after smooching Marv something outrageous and handing him coffee he gulped down in one go. "You shouldn't be doing no heavy lifting."

"I am better now."

Thaddeus agreed, "She's right, Mildred. Think of our boy. Go home and rest. I'll be there right quick. I'll be needing a piping-hot bath something desperate—and a piping-hot coffee like my brother got from his wife."

"I will do that."

Eve mouthed, *You have to tell him!*

I thought of Todd.

I set up Thaddeus's bath in the living room, heart heavy knowing my chores increased tenfold with the man's return. I boiled water in the same large pot I had made the party chowder in that previous fall, the same pot I had washed the bloody mattress pad and sheets in weeks before.

Before I was ready, Thaddeus trudged up the porch stairs and into the house.

"My house is a mess!"

"Thaddeus?" I held a blue towel in my left hand, a new bar of soap in my right.

"What did you do while I was gone? Looks like nothing!"

"I...I taught at school. The usual."

"The laundry is not finished."

"I know, I...I was working on lessons. And other things. The house, it is clean and well organized, I have been working!"

"I am the man in the house, you know, even if am gone. You need to keep up. We're almost to winter!"

A black weight resettled, stone-hard, on my shoulders. "Yes, Thaddeus."

"You tell them students no school until you can catch up at home."

"Why, Thaddeus, I cannot do that!"

He pushed me then, again, like before! I staggered, grabbed a chair for balance, and wondered what he had heard after I left.

"Don't you ever talk back to me again, am sick of it!"

I held my arms across my chest. I was going to yell at him, planned to, but, "Yes, Thaddeus" was all I got out.

Tucking myself as small as I could inside the big square kitchen, I hoped Thaddeus would see I was busy and disappear himself.

He did not.

Hours later, he still lurked about, and then beside me.

Thaddeus lowered himself to one knee and took my hand. "Mildred, my love, forgive me. I was a boor. I am back now. I love you. You can teach all you want. I will care for you and our little one always."

With that, the man tenderly tapped my stomach.

"You will not ever push me around again?"

"Absolutely not."

"Or anything else bad?"

"Well, I can't rightly promise."

"You know what I mean. To me."

"I...sort of promise. I mean, what if I don't know something's bad to do?"

"How can you not know what is wrong or right? And obviously pushing is wrong!"

"Mildred? Please...please forgive me. Dead wrong I was, I know it now."

"You should have known it then."

"Truly sorry. From my heart, I am begging you! Don't know what got into me. Damn prison messed me up before, and I felt all jailed up again out there on Hell Again Island—may as well been prison! Damn sick of even my best friends. Jesus, those men can yap about nothing all the damn night! Anyway, I didn't hit you. Have never hit you."

"You still hurt me."

"I know, am sorry for it. Especially so, I mean, our child...how could I? I am so sorry. Mildred, how many times you want me to say sorry?"

"Hurting me must never, ever happen again. I have got to be sure. Of not hurting. Go take your bath."

"Yes, ma'am."

I focused on the chicken. Thaddeus did as he was told. The man truly stunk, as in fish-so-old-the-edges-of-their-fins-were-green stunk.

The evening wandered into something late before I could set supper on the table. "I tried to make this hen tender, but she is tough. I have been cooking her all evening. I should have picked out a smaller one, but it was big old Hilda that stopped laying."

"Looks some delicious, she does. Been eating lobster and deer all these weeks, would eat a raw snake right now and be happy about it."

I watched Thaddeus shovel large chunks of leathery fowl into his mouth. I would never get used to his wolfing food down like that. But I could live with unmannered eating. Pushing me about? Absolutely not.

"I will count my blessings," I heard myself say aloud.

"What?"

"Oh! We should say a blessing."

"If you like. Don't believe in such things myself. But I will say one anyway."

"How nice! Be my guest."

"Bless this table, and our baby boy."

"Thaddeus."

"Don't argue. Is going to be a boy, I tell you. Don't want no girl. Not the first time around anyways."

"We are not going to have a girl."

"Glad you finally agree with me."

"Or a boy. Our baby. Is gone. We lost the baby."

Thaddeus scowled, stuffed the last bit of chicken into his mouth, threw down his fork with a clatter, and stood up.

"*You* lost the baby!" he hollered, pointing at me. Then he walked out, slamming the door behind him so hard the house rattled.

We said nothing more to each other that evening.

51

Dolphin

After a night of no words or touches, I woke with him inside me. "You did not ask!"

"Got to hurry this," he said through heavy breaths. "We only have a few months to make another, or the darn thing could be born in winter."

"Thaddeus, for the love of God, stop!"

"Not stopping. And be quiet. This ain't working so well."

I closed my eyes, transported myself to Todd's tiny living room with the two bare chairs, holding his hands in mine.

Finally, it worked for him. Thaddeus jumped out of bed the second he was through.

He left in light snow to sell lobsters to Captain Sprague of the schooner *Bountiful,* tied between the deeper water dolphin and stone wharf.

I got my day back.

As well as the strength to confront him.

52

"Thaddeus Francis Gale!" I demanded, hands on my hips, standing by the kitchen door leading to the porch.

Thaddeus leaned against the countertop and folded his arms.

"What now?"

"I am cutting you off."

"What?"

"Like you said this morning, we are too close to next winter if I get pregnant now. Spring babies are better. We will wait. You will wait."

He was about to argue, but my steely eyes met his, and he replied, "That's why I wanted to marry you, Mildred, so as there'd be someone to stand up to me. Not like my...my...um..."

"Not like who?"

"My ma."

"You've never talked about her."

"For a reason."

"I would have liked to meet her."

"I would've liked to know her longer."

"Oh dear. How old were you when she passed?"

"Eight."

The number sliced my heart.

"How terrible! How did she—"

Thaddeus slammed his fist so hard onto the kitchen counter, empty mugs bounced.

"Papa killed her! Went into a rage over supper overcooked, just like Leroy did to Pearl! Attacked her, pushed her into a corner. Pounded on her head. She slumped then, gone. Seconds was all it took. I watched from the table."

"Good Lord!"

"That's what I meant before, when you asked why I married you."

"I do not understand!"

"Needed a wife I would not do that to."

"You've grabbed me hard on the arm. You've pushed me. You forced...took advantage of me, twice now!"

"I know...I *know*! I *hate* myself for all that! But I'm doing better than my pa, ain't I? And you be stronger than my ma. You stand up to me. I need that. Need that bad! Need *you*. I can wait, you know, for the baby making."

I thought of Thaddeus at eight, Orris's age, seeing such horror. But the responsibility of making sure such a thing did not happen again seemed to be on me? That most certainly was not right.

"Did...did your father go to jail, then?"

"No, was an accident. Was, goddamn it! What I remember most is Papa kneeling beside Ma, wailing on like a little baby, and my old man wouldn't never even let me cry. Pa looked at me with bloodshot eyes burning a hole right through my face and said, 'Don't you ever, *ever* do this to a woman, you hear, boy?'

"I promised him then, and we never said another word about it. Pa and I buried Ma behind the house after the constable and fish warden came and wrote up their report. Didn't even have a box. Shoveled dirt across her face first so I could stop looking at it. Pa was so much of a wreck, and there was no family for me to go to, the officers thought it best he stay out of prison. Told him not to worry about it. 'These things happen,' I heard one of them say."

"These things do not just happen! She died! By his hand! He made an eight-year-old bury his mother!"

"I know! Got away with murder, he did! But then he raised me. Who knows where I'd be now if the law hadn't let him off?"

"What about Marvin? He must have been with *his* father. Maybe you could have lived with them. Brothers, after all, should be together."

"Marv was out there somewhere, but we did not know where at the time. His father had left my ma, took Marv and married somebody else."

"I see."

"I feel better now, talking to you like this."

"I don't! Your mother's first husband took her then-only child away. Her second husband killed her in front of her younger son. I want to kill your father myself, I do!"

"He's already dead."

"I want to kill him again."

"You know, Mildred May, need to tell you, my pa, well, he was good for the rest of his life—good to everyone, helped a lot of people, he did. Maybe to make up for what he done. Never got married. Never even went with a woman after that. He loved my ma."

"Funny way to show her, and you. A father's most important job is treating his children's mother well."

"He was wrong. Knew he'd done wrong. Paid for it, too."

I grunted. "She paid more, a lot more. And so did you. And now I am."

"Mildred, please, I forgave my pa. You should, too."

"I am glad you forgave him, is good for you. But I never knew him, and I still hurt from what you have done to me, especially those... those times..."

"When I did not ask?"

"When you did not ask."

"I am sorry. Bottom-of-my-heart sorry. Mildred May, all this talk. I'm plum wore out, feel like a walking dead man right now. Need to go to bed. Join me? I am asking this time."

"Definitely no."

"Goodnight then, Mrs. Mildred May Gale."

"Goodnight."

Thaddeus started to leave, then turned to face me, fire back in his face and gusto in his voice.

"That's why Leroy had to go, I tell you! Was headed that way! Sure as stink! Saw it in him! He was going to do what my pa did to my ma. If I'd been sixteen like Jon instead of eight and gotten to my pa first before he...well, I know this for sure, is right that son of a bitch Leroy is dead."

"Goodnight, Thaddeus."

I stayed up for some time, wondering how the man had managed to get me to feel sorry for him after pushing me into the wall like that. Truth be told, when I stood by the bed and looked at him sleeping, all I could think about was an eight-year-old Thaddeus. No child should ever witness something as monstrous as his own mother getting killed. Even worse was his own father had done the killing.

At least I had bought myself some time. I could not imagine sleeping with that man after his mean shoving, and worse. No matter how much of a hero harbor folk believed him to be, nor how many times he apologized, nor how sad his upbringing was, was not my job to pay for all that.

The harbor could just wait for their precious new baby.

53

The next morning, two weeks before Christmas week, I pulled on the indigo sweater my mother had sent, her consolation gift for not visiting. Todd had left the package on my school desk. The wool was thick, the sweater oversized. Ma had expected me to be pregnant and growing all through winter.

I arrived for class before Lucy, Orris, Irville, and Samuel so I could load up the potbelly stove. I pulled papers out from the day before and stacked them on my desk. Every student had improved his or her writing since the fall term! Every student had jumped in math! They all had become better artists. We rotated drawings in the students' frames constantly. I was so very happy and content in my little schoolhouse of four.

I looked about a room that could comfortably hold six more students. We even had the desks for them. Yet, if I took more than two years to have a child, there would be no children in the school when Lucy graduated eighth grade.

Not a one.

The school would close. And we would need ten to reopen it.

It took nine months for a baby after conception, longer really, depending on how one counted. I had barely a year to be successfully pregnant again.

"Pish-tosh!" I said aloud. "Time enough."

The children arrived, each one also dressed in an oversized, brightly colored sweater.

"Nice sweater, Mrs. Gale."

"Thank you, Orris. My mother knitted it for me."

Orris grasped the front of his sweater with pride.

"My ma made my mine, too. Said I could wear it for three years if I tried not to grow too fast."

"Very handsome."

"What is today's writing assignment?" asked Irville.

I was thrilled with Irville's question. The boy had never hankered much for writing.

"Well, Mr. Thomas, what would you like to write about?"

"How about the person we most admire, our hero?"

"Outstanding! Children, start writing. No shares. Pick your own person. He or she can be alive, or dead, from nearby or far away, famous or generally unknown. You have fifteen minutes. Write small to save paper. And as always, print neatly."

The children scrambled for pencils and precious paper. I turned my attention to Todd's bookshelf, once again admiring its smooth lines and the rich, dark shine he had given it with many thin layers of varnish. I dusted the top and shelves, removing books and artwork for a thorough job.

Samuel finished too quickly and then played tic-tac-toe with himself on the back of the paper. Some minutes later, I stood at the front of the class, surveying the room.

"How about a run outside in that glorious sunshine while I look over your work?"

The children scampered, Lucy and Orris putting on gloves and hats along with their coats. The screen door slammed behind Samuel, the last to go out.

I picked Irville's first:

Mr. Thadius Gale is my hiro.

My Pa werks with him and they ketch alot of lobsters. All ways ketchin alot. My Ma says becus of Thadius we have a nice life here with lots of food and all. Am grapeful Mr. Gale is here.

Why, this was fine! My heart swelled with pride for the two men Irville wrote about, despite so many errors in my oldest student's spelling and grammar. I kept reading:

Am so happy he killed that fella.

The short sentence struck me like the dull end of a hatchet.

Mr. Jenings was no good, says my Ma. Now he is gone. Heard Thadius kelled him that day. Herd my folks tak about it whispring all nite when he was rested. Glad he not in the jale. He did a hiro thing. No jale for him even if found the body I say!

Now our harbor is nicer.

That is why I admire Mr. Thadius Gale and he is my biggest hiro.

Irville's piece was not appropriate writing. Yet, I always told the students they were safe to write their feelings confidentially and without judgment. I had to keep that promise. I only marked spelling and grammar, ignoring my urge to tell him he was wrong.

I picked up Samuel's:

I am my hero. Depending on self not Irv, pa or ma, nobudy no how. Thats realy all to say abaut it.

Good old Samuel! Not much of an effort but well to the point. Orris, who "don't like writing one bit," what would he say? He wrote in big letters on both sides. I lost a tear or three while reading:

My Ma is my hiro. She takes care of me. She always tride to stop Pa. Even when he hirt her. She new he would hirt her and she wood still pretect me. Mommy will always be my hero.

And finally, Lucy's:

Harriet Quimby is my hero. She is the ferst woman to get a pilot lisins! And not last nether, a few more have since Miss Quimby. I will be one. Fly I must. Fly I will. How would the world look, with me hovring above? Small, I expet, yet puir and good and from there I could see everything wrong and right.

Miss Quimby flew across the English Chanel this year. My Mother says Harriet's feet not noticed because the Titanic just sanked. Yes that was terble, but flying the chanel should be top nooz!

I will be top nooz some day. Flying somewhere. Maybe India. Or Africa. Some place far and big. Bigger than here.

Harriet Quimby is my hero, because she tried something big and I want to be big.

Wish she did not die in that crash.

After recess, I made my speech:

"Well now, your papers...as promised, I have only marked them according to spelling and punctuation."

I continued, looking mostly at Irville, "As to content, some of you have very active imaginations, and that is all I am going to say about that."

The three boys and one girl looked at each other, wondering which of them their teacher was referring to. I hoped that Lucy knew I had not meant hers to be too fanciful, and reminded myself to tell her so in private. That girl had to keep her highest dreams in sight.

"By the way, *hero* is spelled h-e-r-o."

Lucy and Samuel jumped for glee while Irville glared at Sam.

"A visitor!" yelled Orris, throwing his hands up in the air.

"It's Mr. Calderwood!" squealed Lucy.

"Mrs. Gale's boyfriend!" added Samuel.

Irville shot Sam an astonished look faster than I could.

"Mr. Thomas! You go straight to the corner for that outrageous outburst!"

I had never sent anyone to the corner before, and it surprised me as much as it did the students.

Todd entered, took off his gray cap and looked around. "Is everything all right?"

"All very well. Right, children? Samuel was just a little bit out of line, but he is fixing himself up nicely now."

"I see that." Todd glanced at the corner where Sam stood. "I could come another time."

"Now is fine."

"I wanted to see how the shelves are working out. Well, I'll be! Look at that stunning art brightening up those plain shelves."

Lucy picked up hers with two hands. "Do you like my lioness?"

"Why yes, she is exquisite."

"How about my night sky?" asked Orris.

"Superb."

"My lobster boats?" asked Irville.

Todd leaned over and studied the boat sketch. Thaddeus, Irville Senior, Marvin, and Jon stood in two boats side by side, each man with exaggerated stern expressions on their round faces.

"Outstanding."

"What about me?" cried Samuel from the corner.

We all laughed.

"Okay, Mr. Thomas. I have no heart to keep you there any longer."

Todd peered at Samuel's drawing of his mother working the small garden by their house. Her shoulders were bent ever so slightly while she hoed, a red scarf on her head, a few birch trees behind in an open field. The likeness to reality was striking.

Todd put his arm on the boy's shoulder. "Incredible. Truly incredible."

"Well, now! Mr. Calderwood just described your work as exquisite, superb, outstanding, and incredible. What do you all think of that?"

"He said mine was '*truly* incredible.'"

"Indeed, you are correct, Samuel. And now there is time for another outdoor runabout to clear everyone's heads for the math quiz."

The children put on their jackets and ran outside. Orris took the wooden hoop and rolled it down the road, the other three laughing as they chased. Todd and I watched from the edge of the boulder on which the schoolhouse was built.

"How has your morning been, Mildred? The children. They are delightful!"

"They are. But my morning has been disappointing."

"How so?"

"A writing assignment. Irville made Thaddeus out to be some kind of hero, because he thinks he killed Leroy."

Todd frowned. "That is not a good message."

"I know. This concerns me."

A pause, and that comfortable silence between us. Again I stopped myself from reaching for his hand. I needed his friendship, but I was married. It was so very lonely trying to have both.

"Mildred, I don't think there's anything you can do about their ideas. That is, without revealing what we know about Jon and Pearl. What would that truth do to poor Orris?"

"We are so trapped in the lie to protect others."

"Exactly so."

"Feels good to be able to talk about it, at least."

"Yes, there is that."

"After losing the baby and all, well, I do not feel obliged to talk to the women, about anything, and I could not very well reveal what Jon did anyway, because only Jon, Pearl, Thaddeus, you, and I know about Jon's role in Leroy's death. And Pearl and Jon do not know we know. And Thaddeus does not know you know!"

"That is certainly complicated enough to not let anyone else in on the secret. I am sorry to hear that about the women, though. They are all you have."

"I have you."

"I am a man."

"I know that, Todd."

"You need women friends. Every gal does, is my understanding."

"You do not seem to have any male friends."

"I do not. Is why I...well, I am rather alone here in Hale, to be honest."

"It is tough when everyone else is married except Rufus?"

"Suppose so."

"Rufus is definitely not much like you."

"I like him fine. We just do not have much in common."

"Just as the other women are not a lot like me. Which is why you are my best friend."

I looked at the children. They huddled together, Lucy pointing at Todd and me, one hand covering her mouth.

"Your students. They may imagine things. I'm afraid they are going to talk at home about my visits."

"Anybody can visit the school, there is nothing wrong in that."

"Maybe there is."

"Everyone knows people will talk about nothing here on the island."

"Still—"

"Well, I have got to give them a test anyway. Do not worry about me, Todd, I can handle the chatter. I worry more about other things."

"Mildred?"

"Yes?"

"You are my best friend, too, something I have missed on Popplestone Isle all these years. I just…just can't stay away from you."

I nodded, and then stood up to call the children, instead hearing high-pitched shrieks before the world turned black.

54

"Mildred you damn fool, I had to come in before hauling our last stretch because of your shenanigans! If we don't get them traps out now, they'll be lost forever. You trying to drain us bone dry?"

"Mr. Gale—Thaddeus—it's not her fault!"

"Shut up!"

"I can understand your concern, but—"

"Said *SHUT UP*, Calderwood. I'll handle my woman from here. Get out of my house."

"I'll be all right, Todd—Mr. Calderwood. I'm fine. Losing the baby and all may be draining me a bit still."

"Don't talk about that!"

"Thaddeus, please!" begged Todd.

"You still here?" Thaddeus turned to Todd, fists clenched. He pulled one arm back, ready to punch.

Todd looked at me, fear mixed with helplessness in his eyes.

"Go!" I ordered.

When Thaddeus turned to me, Todd mouthed behind his back, without a speck of sound, *I am so sorry.*

Thaddeus whirled back around. "Get OUT."

Todd slowly put on his cap and said, "I'll...be going...now."

He headed for the front door at a sloth-like pace while Thaddeus fumed.

As soon as Todd left the porch, Thaddeus commanded, "I forbid you from seeing Calderwood!"

"Forbid me? How about, 'What can I do to make you feel better, Mildred?'"

"What I can do for you is set more rules around here. No seeing other fellas, for one, if you can call him that, behind my back."

"I am not seeing anyone behind your back!"

"In front then. Even worse."

"Todd is a friend, is all. He dropped by the school to see how his bookshelves were working out."

"Not what it looks like."

"What does it look like?"

"Looks like me being made a damn fool of!"

"We are not. I am not. You are not."

"*Hummpph!* I'm going back for the rest of them traps we couldn't get before heading to Hell."

"Where are the children?"

"All home. You just fainted. Never had something like this happen to me, it's embarrassing."

"I did not faint on purpose! And this is not about you."

"He carried you the whole damn way. Must've buckled at the knees, skinny guy like that loaded up with the likes of you."

I rolled over, facing the back of the couch. I would not let Thaddeus see my welled-up, teary eyes. I was glad to hear the door slam and he was gone.

Some hours later his slow walk up the stairs woke me. I stayed still as he entered the bedroom.

"Mildred? You awake?"

I did not reply. My heart raced.

Thaddeus took off his clothes and slid under the covers next to me.

"I'm not always good, but I mean to be. Can be. Will keep trying."

I started to reach for his hand, but pulled it back when he added, "Sure would be better around here though if you got yourself pregnant and stopped being so weak and stubborn."

55

I served the boys their afternoon coffee in the kitchen. They leaned against the counter, backs to the sea, steam rising from dark mugs. Marvin, Jon, and Irville had just spent another mid-December weekend dragging logs down Osprey Hill with Thaddeus.

"I tell you, Mildred, that hill is so damn steep, them oxen poop on their own horns on the way down!"

"Pish-tosh, Thaddeus, please do not engage in such vulgar talk. And you know darn well oxen cannot defecate on their own horns."

"Damn close, is some steep up there. I know a new word for shitting now, thank you, Mildred."

The men laughed and I playfully swatted Thaddeus with a hand towel. "You are infuriating! Well, I am just glad you are all back safe and sound. I do not need further descriptions of an oxen's digestive escapades."

"You sure talk like a teacher," observed Jon.

"That I do. That I am."

"Your ma coming to visit before winter sets in?" asked Marvin.

"I am disappointed to share she is not. She is too busy with the younger ones. And the fishing over there did not go well this year, so she has taken on knitting horse nets."

"Horse nets?"

227

"To keep flies off. Horse netting is big on Crescent now. My mother is one of many making them. They cannot work fast enough to meet the demand in New Hampshire and Massachusetts especially."

"Some funny to be making horse nets instead of fishing nets on an island," said Marv. "Hey, maybe Min could do that."

"Min could. My ma knits fishnets too, but more horse nets these days. An odd combination, I agree. She would much rather be knitting socks and sweaters. She would *much* rather be knitting baby blankets."

"Reckon so. Maybe she can visit in the summer," encouraged Marv.

"I hope so."

Thaddeus tapped my stomach for all to see and said, "Perk up, Mrs. Gale. A baby will come along soon."

Jon was uncharacteristically talkative. "Will be mighty nice having a little one in the harbor again."

"Sure will," added Marvin.

"But I am not pregnant."

"You will be," insisted Marvin. "Have to make up for Min and me."

"Oh Marv, that's nobody's fault! I so tire of hearing about this."

Thaddeus bristled and all eyes followed his. Todd, whistling again and hands in his trouser pockets, was ambling across the lawn toward the porch.

Todd took a step back as Thaddeus opened the door before Todd could even knock. "Oh, Mr. Gale, how are you?"

"Ummpph."

Todd looked at me, wondering, it seemed, how to reply. I shrugged. He then quite deliberately walked over our threshold into the kitchen.

Irv, Marv, and Jon stood still as beach boulders as Thaddeus demanded, "What brings you to my home?"

"Well, I...I was just going to look for mushrooms. They are quite rare but do appear this time of year and wondered if Mrs. Gale and you would like some."

"You mean pay you for them?"

"Why no! On me. My pleasure. Matsutakes make for quite a healthy soup."

"Matsu— what?"

"The name comes from Japan. They are more generally known as pine."

"So just say pine."

"Yes, sir," Todd replied, and I cringed.

"We don't take no charity."

"Not charity. Neighborly gift, is all. Would you like some?"

"We would like some, thank you, Mr. Calderwood," I stammered before my husband could jump in.

Todd tipped his red cap and left.

"Don't like him."

Marvin chuckled. "Think he knows that, Thaddeus."

"I do not see why you all do not like him," I admonished. "He is a fine fella, he is."

Irville laughed. "Mighty fine and dandy, sure is that."

I boiled hot all of a sudden, terribly annoyed they acted like jackasses. "What is that supposed to mean?"

"Nothing, Mildred, nothing. I am sorry," said Irville. "You are right, Todd is a good fellow. Very nice indeed."

"He's a Brownie!" Thaddeus chimed in with a little boy's voice.

"Thaddeus!"

"Don't like him hovering around my house."

"This is my house, too!"

Thaddeus frowned and squinted at me, and then, to my relief, said calmly, "You're right, Mildred. Some ways this house be more yours with all them frilly curtains on the windows. You talk to Calderwood, though, when I'm not here, needs to be on the porch."

"Naturally."

"Okay then. You boys going to stand around here gawking or what?"

Irville, Marvin, and Jon darted out the door, Jon tripping on his own feet, caught by Marv before the boy would have hit the floor.

Thaddeus turned on me then, dark eyes in force. Before I could say anything, he put his large hands on my shoulders and shoved me against the kitchen wall. "Don't you *ever* cross me again in front of my friends. Understand?"

The air was knocked right out of me. I could not speak.

"Understand?"

"Yes," I finally whispered.

"Well, I'm some starving. Get supper on the table."

Despite my trembling, I felt more fury than fear. I did not even care if he went so far as to hit me! I almost wished he would, so there would be proof of the hurt that so far stayed rock-hard under my skin. Then I got my breath back.

"Do not *ever* touch me like that again!"

Thaddeus cackled.

"You think this is funny? You do anything to me, I am gone. I will leave for Crescent, with a baby inside me if I am pregnant, and there will be no other child here to help recover the harbor. And no teacher for the others, either!"

That was all pure bluffing. I could not go back to my parents' home, nor could I ever leave Lucy, Orris, Samuel, or Irville. Truth be told, I could not stand the thought of leaving Todd. I had nowhere to go.

I added, "Understand?"

Thaddeus lowered both hands, then turned and walked away without a sound.

56

Thaddeus sulked for nearly a week. Not a word in private, just little grunts and nods when I offered him soup, donuts, cheese, anything. I was living with a toddler's never-ending temper tantrum, the boy middle-aged.

Yet when Marvin, Irville, or Jon came by, Thaddeus would kiss me on the cheek and say, "Have a good day, my Mrs. Gale."

Always the perfect gentleman, he was, in front of others.

I was at wit's end by the Saturday before Christmas.

When Thaddeus walked into the kitchen that afternoon, I stomped my feet and yelled, "Thaddeus Francis Gale!"

He kept walking.

"No more supper fixings unless you talk to your wife!"

Thaddeus pulled off his bait-encrusted hat and sighed. "After my bath."

The complicated man had finally spoken.

"Mildred May?"

"Yes?"

"Please come here."

I dropped my apron, re-clipped a wooden barrette in my hair, and entered the living room.

Thaddeus reached out a wet hand, extending it to mine.

I took it.

"Join me, please."

"We need to talk first."

"I would like to talk second. I...I'll be nice this time, a promise."

"But we will talk."

"Promise to, yes."

I locked the front door and dropped my outer clothes as he watched, took off my brassiere, exposing unwieldy breasts filling my torso. They hurt, that time of the month coming, so I held them up with my hands.

"I like what you're doing."

"I like that you like what I am doing."

I did. It had been a long time. To be honest, I had missed the lovemaking.

With one arm tucked underneath my breasts I slid my intimates off with the other. Thaddeus licked his upper lip. He let out a cricket-like sound.

I managed to stand on the little stool and put one leg over the rim of the tub. I let my breasts go so I could hold on with two hands, and then awkwardly slid into the bath.

The water rose and sloshed over the top.

"My word, am I that large?"

"Floor needed a good washing anyway."

"I did not know I would displace so much of it."

"You are an ample woman, Mildred. Ample and able."

"You appreciate me."

"We were going to talk afterwards, was the deal."

"Yes, that would be fine."

I kissed him.

"Like your kisses. Keep them coming."

"I like that you like my kisses, I will keep them coming."

"Not waiting for a spring baby instead? You see, I am asking now."

"We are not waiting. Thank you for asking."

We kissed for a while. He had to be what I desired, for there was no other.

"I need you to be mine," I heard myself say. We got closer, arms and bodies wrapped in the tub, but I was not ready to forgive all the wrongs.

"'Course I be yours. Who else's would I be?"

"I like how you say that, Thaddeus."

"Not complicated. I be yours. You be mine."

"Yes, I guess."

"You guess?"

"Sometimes you are...not really you, not your best you, I am sure of it."

He stopped. "So we are talking now?"

"Yes, please, I hope so."

"Am no good sometimes, I know that, Mildred. Working on that. Hope you can be patient with me. This is really a promise to you."

"I hope I can be patient. I like who you are, right now. I would like you to be this all the time."

"Can't sit in the tub all the time."

"You know what I mean, Thaddeus."

"Think I do. How do you want me to be?"

"I want you to be the man I can love all the time. Or at least most of the time. No, all of the time."

"How do I do that?"

"Be kind."

"I can do kind."

"Caring."

"I care."

"Honest."

"I am honest."

"Really? All the time?"

"Um, well maybe I can try to be honest."

"Well now, 'maybe I can try' is more honest of you!"

"You see, am getting there."

"Honest and kind, all of the time, is what I want and need, is what I need very badly."

That fella's eyes softened then to something I had not seen before. I felt hope. That hope felt fine.

"Mildred, I will try hard for everything you want. Just be clear what you want."

"I prefer a promise, but trying hard is an acceptable start."

"Can we stop talking now?"

"Yes, dear." I stroked his wet hair.

And then the floor got its washing.

57

Thaddeus left early the following morning. As I lay in bed half asleep, he whispered, "I love and appreciate you, Mrs. Gale. That's more of the talk I promised."

A few hours later, I balanced a mug of coffee on my plate and opened the door with my free hand, the weather warm enough even in late December for breakfast on the porch.

"Good morning, Mildred."

Todd startled me more than I could understand. Hearing his voice and seeing his kind smile made me feel untethered, alone, and oddly guilty.

"I saw Orris in his yard playing and realized I had my days off. Thought it was Monday, but it is Sunday," he continued.

"A Sunday before Christmas, no less!" My response came out in an embarrassing shriek.

"Mildred, what's the matter!" Todd scrambled up the porch, sat in the chair next to me, and wiped my tears.

"I do not know what has gotten into me!"

"You need to take better care of yourself."

"But I am. Look at the size of this breakfast."

"Which you have not yet taken a bite of, surely part of your problem."

Todd leaned to me, picked up my fork, cut some egg white and runny yolk, and brought the wet concoction to my mouth. I took a slow, savory bite.

A surge of balance and normalcy ran through me.

"Thank you, Todd. I am so absurd."

"Not absurd. You are a special woman going through a lot, is all."

"You do not know why I am blubbering."

"Why are you?"

"I cannot even tell you." I did not even know for sure myself.

"I see."

Todd continued to feed me, his hand caressing the back of my neck with one thumb, making me feel better and worse at the same time.

I broke off some bread and dipped it into the river of yolk.

"Are you hungry, Todd?"

"A bit."

I brought the bread to his mouth. The pull on it as he took the first bite made me feel things.

We did not speak until finishing the meal, ever so slowly.

"Mr. Gale is a lucky man," Todd said softly.

"Perhaps."

"Does...does he—oh, never mind, my goodness!"

"What?"

"Not my place to ask."

"Todd."

"Yes?"

"You can ask me anything."

"I will. Does Thaddeus treat you right at home?"

I looked out across the harbor, beyond the ledge I had last drifted by on my wedding day in a peapod, seasick, six months previous. I thought about the precious night before with Thaddeus, and then of the horrific time when he came home from Rockland. I reached under the table for Todd's hand, enveloping it with both of mine.

"Not always, but usually."

Todd placed his other hand over my grasp.

"The usually needs to be always."

"I wish so, too."

"Is that why you were crying?"

"What in heaven's name!" A woman's voice.

Todd shifted his seat to the left and pushed my hand away.

"Did you see that crazy-looking deer?" asked Eve, coming into sight from around the back side of the porch.

"No," I replied, relieved Eve could not have seen how close Todd and I had been. How could I be so careless? It was not even a foggy day!

"Oh, Mr. Calderwood, good morning to you, too."

Todd coughed. "Good morning. Are you talking about that half-white doe?"

"Wonder if the meat's any different."

"Wouldn't think so," Todd replied. "She's albino. Skin deficiency, is all."

"I see."

"Genetic."

"Whatever that means. Sort of pretty. What are you two up to?"

"Was out for a walk, saw Mildred here on a rare day off, and stopped by to say hello."

"A walk? In December?"

"Why, yes. Like you seem to be on, Eve."

"I was wondering how Mildred was doing also. Still feel good, dear?"

"Yes, I do."

"Good. Means more likely to...well, never mind that now." She looked at Todd and then back at me. "I'd stay, but I have such a pile to do."

"Thank you for stopping by, Eve. Means a lot, really—anytime."

"Mildred, I must go," Todd said as soon as Eve was out of earshot. "Doesn't look right me being by and all."

"I always welcome your company, Todd. I... Well, Thaddeus is not so welcoming to you. I am so sorry about him."

"He doesn't like me. I wish he did. I could see you more often then."

"He could like you."

"He hates me now."

"Hate is such a strong word. I do not allow that word in my schoolroom."

"I mean nothing by anything, really. I care for you, is all. I am no threat to Mr. Gale, not at all! He and you must know that."

"Please call him Thaddeus. He is younger than you."

"Thaddeus, then. I mean no threat to Thaddeus."

"I know that." Accepting Todd's assurance flooded me with disappointment.

"Anyway, he could crush me in moments." Todd's voice sounded humored, not quite terrified, yet perhaps a little afraid.

"That he could."

"He needs to treat you right, Mildred. Always, not usually!"

"He will. I am working on that. And I will try to bring him around to being nicer about you. No reason a man and a woman cannot be friends."

"That's right. No law against that."

"Exactly."

"Just harbor gossip."

"There is that."

"And a wife should not have to work on her husband being nicer."

"I know, but seems I do."

58

That Monday before Christmas Eve, the snow draped the low-tide flats and shores. Was as if a giant white kitchen tea towel softly lay upon Hale, muffling the harbor.

Sea smoke rose in gentle wisps and then in thick cloudlike bursts across the harbor and beyond. Although bitterly cold and deathly quiet, looked like a roaring fire was upon the water all the way to the horizon.

"Goddamn weather!" Thaddeus stood, hands on his bare hips looking out over the wintry harbor.

"Thaddeus, my word. Anyone walks by, they will see you in all your birthing-day glory."

"Ain't nobody going to be walking by today. Too cold."

"Suppose you are right."

"I am always right about this harbor. Should be named Gale, not Hale."

I rolled out of bed, bare feet on icy floorboards. Tiptoed to Thaddeus's side.

He put his arm around my waist.

"You are so warm, Thaddeus, am surprised steam isn't rising off of you."

"Sea is flat, am going out. Still got to haul in one last load of pots."

"Be careful. She could change, you know that better than anybody. And you can barely see anything with all that sea smoke."

"That's right. I know better than anybody. Don't go worrying yourself. Seas will stay calm for the day. And that sea smoke will be gone soon as the sun's higher."

"Let me fix you a nice breakfast first."

"You do that."

Thaddeus inhaled his scrambled eggs and warm bread in seconds and then joined the boys.

I waited at school for an hour before realizing students were not going to show up. I rushed home to do what I could about the first snowfall on Popplestone. The way people were acting, seemed they expected far worse than Crescent ever got hit with.

59

I started with shoveling a path to the barn directly under the clothes-line. Attached to the line was a rope with a large loop at both ends we would hold onto heading to the outhouse in a whiteout storm.

Path complete, I gathered small logs from the woodpile inside the barn for the house cookstove and potbelly.

I nearly ran into Todd with my second load. "My goodness, you startled me!"

"I've finished my chores and figured you and Thaddeus had a lot to do. He's fishing. May I help, please?"

"Yes, thank you."

We made short work of the woodpile, Todd carrying loads to the doorway and me bringing them inside. In twenty minutes, the house had enough for the week.

Next we cleaned the chicken shed behind the house, scooping the old hay into the summer compost beyond the barn.

We then took the table and chairs off the porch and put them in the barn. I brought boots from the porch into the house, placing them upside down on a towel to drain out the snow, while Todd moved fishing gear piled up on the porch to the barn workshop.

He beamed through every chore like he was enjoying it.

"You by my side, Todd, is such a joy."

"For me, too. Mr. Gale will not be angry?"

"Better Thaddeus does not know."

Todd raised one eyebrow. "That may be wise. I am not insulting him, am I?"

"I don't mean to take credit for your work, but, well, at the moment, um, is best if he thought I did all this myself."

"One could easily believe you did."

"Thaddeus is a challenge, I guess you know that. I am still learning about him."

"He expects a lot. Too much."

"Suppose he needs to."

"Island life?"

"Island life."

The snow continued to fall in what looked like weightless diamond crystals. The sky burst into a bright blue between ivory clouds layered across the sky. A few seagulls crossed the harbor looking for food, or eagles to harass.

Todd paused to take in the harbor scenery. "I never tire of the beauty here."

"Nor do I. The barn roof is a pretty white with all that snow."

"Like a wedding cake."

"Indeed. Um...Todd? What does Thaddeus do in the winter, do you know?"

"I forget this is only your first year here."

"First year. First winter."

"Well, I...ah..."

"Oh my, you sound nervous. What does he do?"

"Um. You know, I hope—well maybe he won't this year. A married man can be completely different. Usually is."

"Won't what?"

"Well, in the past, I mean, sometimes, he goes for the rum. Sometimes whiskey. Or both. Has parties. The music is splendid! Marv plays the accordion, Irville the mandolin, and Thaddeus, well, he sings while strumming a ukulele or plays the harmonica. I can hear them all the way from my house, especially so when there is thick fog. I have always enjoyed their playing."

"And the drinking?"

After a pause Todd said, "Too much of that."

"Oh."

"Mildred?"

"Yes?"

"You need any help, remember, come running. Will you if you need to? Run to me?"

"I will."

"Good. I best be going now. Make sure your fisherman knows you did all this work, now."

"I will."

Moments after Todd left, Mineola came by.

My sister-in-law walked right into my house without knocking, yanked off her hat, and announced, "You are playing with fire, Mildred May Gale!"

60

"Thaddeus is mighty good to this harbor, you know," Min continued harshly. "Don't cross him."

"What are you talking about?"

"Everything."

"Min, what is going on?"

"I'd like to ask you the very same question!"

"I have no idea what you are talking about."

"I saw him."

"Who?"

"Todd Calderwood. Here."

"For goodness sake, Min, Todd helped me load firewood. The man did not even come into the house, but he could, is my house. Everyone seems to agree Todd is sweet on men, you and Eve said so right here in my kitchen!"

"Seems sweet on *you*. Maybe he don't go for men like we thought."

"Staying or going, Min? Going means you are still accusing me and not sorry. I would prefer you stay."

Min stood there, looked out to sea, back at me, arms crossed, fingers tapping. "You are one tough woman. I...I'd like to stay."

"Well, that is more like it!"

I put my arm around her. "Harbor is too small for fighting. Time for a donut?"

Min took off her coat and mittens. "I do. Mildred, I'm sorry. Is just that, well, you know, Thaddeus is Marvin's boss. And they are brothers, after all."

"Thaddeus can look after himself, we all know that. We women need to stick together, remember? You are the one who first told me that."

"That's right."

Min sat quietly, picking at the donut I placed in front of her, forehead creased something fierce.

"Min, what is on your mind?"

"It's Thaddeus. Mildred, he will be so jealous. No telling what he'll do if he sees you and Todd together. Maybe that's why I was so sharp—am more worried about you than looking out for him. Sometimes, you know, Thaddeus, he, um..."

"Goes for the rum. Or whiskey."

"Uh-huh."

"I expect that. There will be more drinking when there's no fishing to keep him busy."

"Just so."

"I am going to try to have him drink less."

"Good idea. Might be difficult."

"Maybe Marvin and Irville can help?"

"They make it worse."

"Oh."

"Thing is, Marv and Irv don't get mean when they drink. They get floppy and goofy and unbelievably stupid. And Marv gets very... well, let's just say I don't mind his drinking one bit. But Thaddeus, the man gets mean."

"Oh."

"Feel like I have to warn you. And then there's...well, I feel like I have to defend him, too! You're the only one around here who don't seem to understand Thaddeus is our hero."

"Hero?" *I was right tired of hearing that. First a student, then Eve, and Min, too!*

"With Leroy gone and all."

"Thaddeus had nothing to do with Leroy's disappearance."

"My Marv says your Thaddeus got away with murder. We owe Thaddeus for that."

"Nobody owes him anything. Anybody *see* him kill Leroy?"

"No."

"Rumors."

"Maybe."

"Just rumors."

"Okay, could be that Thaddeus just told Leroy to get out of town or he'd end up dead. Still makes Hale better. As long as Leroy ain't here, the how don't matter none."

"Thaddeus has not told me anything about Leroy," I lied.

"To protect you."

"No, because there is nothing."

"But...but if Thaddeus did kill Leroy, we are some grateful. Leroy was up to no good, would've killed Pearl or Orris eventually. Don't hold it against our Thaddeus."

I looked at Min for what felt like a long time, plum angry that she referred to my husband as the harbor's own, as if I were an outsider meddling things up. Min's brow crinkled up like a little girl's waiting to hear her test grade.

"Nobody knows what happened, and that means my husband is officially innocent!"

"Okay. Okay! You can believe that. I have to go. No dashing older fella come by to help *me* today."

Min put on her coat, hat, and mittens and headed out the door.

"Min wait, one more thing, hate to ask."

"What?"

"Maybe you should not tell Marv or Thaddeus about Todd dropping by. I am going to take credit for all the work around the house. Could you do that for me, please?"

"Was my plan."

"Thank you."

"You're welcome. Be careful."

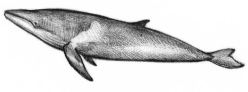

61

Minke whale

"Students, it is Christmas Eve! Only a half day today. Give school work your full attention this morning."

"But Santa is here!" cried Orris.

"That's Mr. Calderwood!" said Lucy, laughing.

"I know, but he's definitely Santa today," insisted Orris.

I looked at Todd standing outside the door. He sported a wig made of what appeared to be white rabbit fur on his head, and the same was somehow stuck to his face for a beard. He wore a red jacket with clumps of white material sewn on to look like buttons and a bright red velvet pointy cap.

I stood, arms crossed.

He opened the door. "Ho-ho-ho?"

"Mr. Calderwood! We were about to start a lesson."

"Oh yes, I see that. I am so very sorry. May I come back later?"

"At the end of school, in three and a half hours."

"Yes ma'am."

The children watched him go and then glumly sank into their chairs.

"We need to use every moment to get each of you ready to graduate to the next class," I commanded.

"Yes, ma'am."

"Yes, ma'am."

"Yes, ma'am."

"Yes, ma'am."

Three hours and forty grueling minutes later, I heard the sweet chorus, "Santa's back!"

"Do come in, Mr. Claus. We are so happy to see you."

"I'm so glad," replied Todd, and then more softly as the children peered into his giant red bag, "I am so sorry, Mildred. Been fretting all morning I'd ruined your lessons. How has it gone?"

"Absolutely fine," I fibbed. "I am the one who needs to apologize for being so sharp. I thought I had scared you off for the day."

"Almost did indeed, but I was already dressed up, so came back."

"Happy you did."

"Santa! Our presents!"

"Yes, Santa at your service!"

Todd held the big red sack with one hand, dramatically reaching in with the other.

He pulled out one brightly wrapped package at a time.

"Now, you all open them at once, so as not to spoil the surprise for the others."

"They are the same?"

"They are similar."

Samuel's fingers twitched as he tugged on the edge of blue paper with white stars like Orris's and Lucy's. Irville eyed his brother's package until he received his own red-and-white-striped one. The four stood in front of Todd, wide-eyed, Orris and Lucy gently biting their lips.

"Okay!"

The students tore the packages open, paper dropping onto the floor.

"Ahhhhh!" Lucy held up her treasure with two hands and danced around the room.

"A coyote!" announced Samuel. "They are so funny and tricky!"

"Coyotes are also very adaptable and can see things others don't, like you do in your art."

Samuel stared at Santa for a moment, and then back at his carving, grinning.

"He's the best," said Irville, brushing his fingers across the smooth surface of his minke whale. The creature appeared to be in movement, its tail curved upward in magnificent fashion.

Orris cupped his in two hands, mouth slightly open, eyes rapidly blinking away tears.

I glanced at Todd, who was also watching Orris. The harbor's youngest boy looked up at Todd and whispered, "Mr. Calderwood, how did you know?"

"Know?"

"This one comes to me in dreams all the time."

"I did not know about your dreams, Orris, but am not surprised. The bear suits you."

"It does? How?"

"Many reasons." Todd paused, seeming to choose his words carefully. "The bear's meaning is to stand up against adversity, be strong and confident, heal, and in healing you can lead and help others."

Orris placed his treasure on the desk so the wise brown bear could stand and stare back at him. "Thank you, Santa."

"Tell me about my bird," demanded Lucy.

"Ahhh, the great blue heron, one who determines her own destiny."

"Hooray for me! And I am going to fly like a heron one day!"

"And the whale?"

"Your whale, Irville, represents the importance of family and community. And he is as strong as he is peaceful."

"Okay, got it. I like that, Mr. Ca— Santa, thanks."

"This is all so fascinating, how do you know all this?" I asked.

"Indians told me."

"Injuns?" asked Irville, looking up from his carving.

"Well, yes, *In...dians.*"

"My pa says Injuns are savages."

Todd glanced at me before he responded, "Well now, Indians are different from us, is all. They hold a great deal of wisdom, including how animals communicate with people, often in dreams. Irville, really, please call them Indians. Or Penobscot or Passamaquoddy, tribes of the Wabanaki that live around here. They are not savages! And Injuns is not right to say, either, not right at all. Indians have lived here well over ten thousand years, after all, long before we arrived."

"Well, if Santa says so."

"Santa says so. Anybody else dream about animals?"

"I do!" added Lucy. "Including the great, great blue heron sometimes!"

I reluctantly interrupted, "This is a wonderful lesson, but we are close to the end of school, another snowfall is coming, and parents need their children at home. Tell you what, Mr. Calderwood can come in after the holidays and talk more about all this, how about that? Oh wait, I should have asked first. I did not mean to presume."

"Speaking before these fine young minds will be my honor."

Lucy giggled. "Never knew Santa talked like that!"

"Pa won't like us learning Injun—Indian—ways," Irville stated solemnly.

I frowned, then replied, "Indians live around here and often come to Hale Harbor. They are neighbors. We should understand them better."

"Yes, ma'am. I guess my pa would be okay with that."

"Santa, your carvings are stunning works of art, thank you," I added.

"Thank you, Santa!" cried the children in unison.

"You are all very welcome. Ah, there is one more."

Lucy clapped her hands. "For our teacher!"

"Yes, for your teacher."

Todd reached into the long sack, hand at the bottom searching corner to corner. His face glanced upwards as he pretended he could not find anything, and then he exclaimed, "A-ha!"

He pulled out a package almost twice as big as the others and handed it to me.

I unwrapped my piece carefully so I could save its bright-orange paper.

"A boat!" the Thomas brothers exclaimed together.

"My oh my—a perfect model of Mr. Gale's fishing peapod!" I exclaimed, placing it on my desk and running my fingers along the side of the white-painted carving.

The children gathered around the desk, eyes wide.

"Look at the herring in a little bait box!" squealed Lucy.

"And a trap and buoy," said Samuel.

"I can imagine Mr. Gale and Pa fishing out of that boat, looks just like the real thing," added Irville.

The treasure included seats in the bow, stern, and middle of a peapod. A string connected a tiny trap made of shavings and a white wooden buoy with a yellow stripe. Long, smooth oars painted white just like Thaddeus's were secured in thin, loosely-wired oarlocks.

"Mr. Calderwood, this is exquisite."

"I hope Mr. Gale likes it as much as you do."

"I am sure he will."

"Like what? And what the *helllll* are you doing here?!"

For the first time ever, Thaddeus had come into my school. We had been too focused on the gift to even notice him stagger in the doorway. And for the first time since that afternoon he threw Leroy Jennings over the railing, he was woefully intoxicated. My heart sank. I feared for Todd, but, thinking of the children first, I stepped out of the way and in front of them, serving poor Uncle Santa up to the mercy of that drunken wolf.

62

Thaddeus took an unbalanced swing at Santa, who slowly ducked as he kept his eyes on his opponent's face. Thaddeus's punch skimmed over the top of Todd's head, silently knocking the red velvet cap off as Thaddeus toppled under his own ungainly weight. He then slid along the shelf, arms flailing, grasping at framed art. He landed on the floor with a deep thud, the children's precious creations clattering about him.

Lucy and Orris shrieked.

"Students! Go home! Irv and Sam get your pa! Run fast!"

As Thaddeus groaned and tried to get up, four children grabbed winter gear, clutched their wooden animals, and tore out the door. After the screen door slammed behind him, Orris peeked back in.

"Will you be all right?"

"Yes!" Todd and I yelled at the same time.

"I'll get Mr. Browne."

"Good idea, Orris!"

"Good idea, Ooorrrissss?" Thaddeus had made it to his feet, entirely unsteady. He shook his head side to side, vomit flying, half of it coating Lucy's desk.

Todd gestured to my chair. "Mr. Gale, have a seat. I'll bring you some tea."

"Not taking any tea from the likes of you! You're one of *those—and* you're after my woman!"

"Thaddeus, that does not make any sense at all!" I cried.

Todd put his hand up to his lips in a shushing signal to me, then whispered, "Mildred, don't. It'll just rile him. He is not going to remember any of this anyway."

I quietly hissed, "Well, I never! That just does not make sense. None of it!"

"You stay away from him!" Thaddeus pointed a long, craggy finger at me, his legs bent and swaying, like he was dancing some newfangled way.

"Mr. Gale, I came by with gifts. Look at this one for your future son or daughter, or for you." Todd held the little boat in front of Thaddeus's face with two hands, almost bowing as he presented it. Thaddeus's sway slowed, eyes squinting up. I watched with my arms crossed, disgusted by how hard it was for that man to focus.

"Well I'll be jiggered!" Thaddeus raised his right hand above the carving, managed to zero in on it, then grabbed and held it carefully. "This here is my boat!"

"Yes, she is."

"Pretty. You make this? What are you dressed up as, anyways?"

"Santa Claus."

"And this here is for my baby boy?"

"Yes, sir."

"Mighty fine, yes, mighty fine. Got to make a baby boy again first, though." My husband eyed me as warily as I scowled back.

I put my hands on my hips, impressed with Todd and furious at Thaddeus. I had never seen anyone turn a drunk into such a kitten. My hulking husband seated himself, boat in his left hand, his right lifting the tiny buoy and throwing it overboard. He then rowed one of the oars.

Thaddeus giggled. "I like this here boat."

I was grateful for an unbelievably stupid drunk over a mean one.

"Mildred, he's too big," Todd whispered. "I'm going to need help getting Thaddeus home."

I nodded to the window. Marvin, with Irville right behind him, was dashing up the stairs.

"Help is here."

"Good."

Marv deftly pulled Thaddeus up by his big arms and supported him from the left as they headed for the door, Irville on his right, their quick actions appearing well practiced.

Marv turned our way. "He'll sleep this off, don't you worry, Mildred. We'll stay with him until he goes down. Best you get home an hour later...er, maybe two is better."

"Thank you both."

Thaddeus dropped the toy boat.

Irville caught it with his free hand. "Nice. You make this, Calderwood?"

"Yes."

"He gave a carving to each of the children, from Santa."

"Much obliged, Todd, on behalf of my boys."

Irville handed the boat to me and said, "Best you keep this for now."

"Thank you again for coming so fast."

"Any time."

"One more favor, Irville."

"Anything, Mildred."

"Please prop Thaddeus up so he stays sleeping on his side. He will be safer that way if he throws up in his sleep."

"We will."

I did not object when Todd joined me in righting the classroom. We went about our chores without speaking.

I mopped the floor and wiped down Lucy's desk while Todd returned the artwork to his bookshelf. Lucy's frame was chipped, but otherwise there was no damage. Todd swept the floor where he could while I mopped. He threw the dust out the back door into the bushes, the same place I squeezed out the mop filled with what Thaddeus had retched. After thoroughly rinsing my hands in the washbowl and dumping its contents, we straightened the desks and chairs.

"Thank you, Todd. You are such a blessed help, again. Having to clean up and your treatment in our school today is much more than you bargained for. And to think you came here as Santa bearing such thoughtful gifts!"

"This is the least I can do, given all the disruption I have caused."

"Thaddeus's drinking is not your fault."

"I know, but he was far from happy to see me here."

"A man drinks, no telling what he will do."

"True."

"He certainly likes your boat."

"I am grateful for that."

"Well, this was all a very easy cleanup, thanks to you."

"Let me walk you home."

"It is still too early, according to Marvin."

"Then come to mine."

63

We made quite the pair. Me a big woman wearing a man's green, full-length winter jacket, he a slender Santa covered in red velvet and white rabbit. Snowflakes silently drifted between and all around us.

We scurried past the Thomas home and looked to the harbor. The sea ran hard that day, her high tide slamming white-capped breakers on the shore under a gray sky.

"I am worried about you, Mildred May."

"Don't be. I am going to find his liquor stash and get rid of it, all of it. Thaddeus is fine s'long as he don't drink. Oh my!"

"What?"

"I promised myself as an island schoolteacher I would always speak properly, even in casual conversations. Let me try again: 'Thaddeus is fine as long as he does not drink.'"

"I understood you both times."

"It is important to me to speak correctly."

"Then it is important to me, as well."

"We are here."

I felt at home in Todd's tiny house smelling of rich coffee and morning-baked bread. Todd's place was one floor, with a small Vermont potbelly stove set in the middle of the entry doubling as a living room. A modest kitchen and single bedroom connected to the main room.

I took off my coat.

He added four sticks of firewood to the potbelly.

"Mildred—"

"I know."

"This must be wrong."

"Being with you feels right, Todd."

"I find myself feeling the same way."

"I know."

Todd brushed his finger down my cheek. I rested my hand on his neck behind his fake beard, thumb caressing his ear. Every ounce of me screamed for him, a desire so overwhelming, an odd discomfort was part of the pleasure.

Todd pulled off his beard, leaned in, and kissed me, long and slow and nice. He tasted of sweet jam, milk with coffee. I wrapped my arms around him and pulled him close. He kissed my neck, barely touching my skin with several tiny pecks.

After a while, I loosened my grip and unbuttoned his red jacket, careful not to damage the Santa accessories. I pushed it off and down his arms, where it hung for a moment. He shook his arms, and the jacket silently dropped to the floor. We stood there for a while, caressing, until he took my hand.

"Mildred, are you sure?"

"I want to, Todd."

"You are married."

"I am not married today."

"Mildred!"

"Let us try for that baby! I want one as much as you do. I would rather have yours. I am agreeing with you, Todd. Listen to me, please...I am agreeing."

"You are sure."

"I am. Are you?"

"Yes. I...you should know I want a child with you. I have been thinking about that for weeks...no...months. Honestly, perhaps ever since I took your hand to help you off the beach your first day here, felt it then. A kind of destiny, perhaps. I have not been able to get the crazy idea out of my mind."

"Then let's."

"We should not," he whispered.

"Please, for me." I took his hand and led him the few steps to the bedroom.

For what Todd lacked in finesse, he made up for with care and love and whispering sweetly into my ear as we held each other close. I could not stop kissing him—his mouth, his nose, his eyelids, and particularly his ears. I enveloped every part of his body, and he accepted everything I did with a rapidly beating heart and repeating, "I love you, Mildred, I love everything about you."

We sometimes paused to lie on the bed, where we talked, holding each other quietly.

We snuggled like that for hours, loving each other the way we could.

"We are not going to, in entirety, are we?" he finally said, running his finger along my bare leg as he kissed my nose. I wore nothing by then. My body wanted him to touch me there, my mind relieved he had not yet dared to.

"I want to, Todd, I really do."

"You are married."

"How did you know?"

"That you are married?!"

"No. How do you know I cannot go through with this, as much as I want to, as much as I...love you."

"You've not removed my drawers. Surely it is obvious I would welcome you to."

"I am sorry."

"Do not be, this is the right thing, to stop."

"But Todd, you want a baby."

"Yes, I do."

"Then maybe we—"

"I will be your child's uncle, not its father."

"The doting uncle you so deserve to be. You deserve so much more."

"I am content with uncle."

"I still care for you, even though we do not, you know..."

"I know you do, Mildred. Me too."

"I wish I could stay here forever, Todd. I do not want to go home."

"I wish so too, but we have much exceeded Marvin's two-hour suggestion. I will walk you home now, unfortunately past Eve's and Min's houses."

64

Todd and I stood next to my porch for some time that windy, snowy afternoon. Truth be told, I regretted not finishing what we had started. I should have taken off his drawers! My body ached in a most horrible fashion, I felt my heart would never slow down, and I longed for his touch upon my face and everywhere else.

We could not even hold hands there, for all the harbor would see.

I finally relented. "I...so hate to go...but I best be getting inside. It is cold. Our stove no doubt needs restarting, and yours needs more wood. And Min is watching us from her window."

Todd nodded. "I'll wait here. Please open the door after you go in and wave if Thaddeus is asleep. If he is awake, come right out and we'll get Marvin."

"I will. The presents today, Todd, they mean so much to the children, and to me, thank you."

"Oh, right, and here is yours."

Todd took the carving out of his pocket, lifted the buoy up and jiggled it so the string unraveled and he could place it inside the peapod.

"I'll put it on the bureau for Thaddeus to see when he awakes."

"Good idea. Oh God, I hate the thought of him with you in the bedroom!"

"I am sorry, Todd. You do not know how sorry I am!"

Once again, I thought about pulling Todd to me and kissing him long and slow, and then bringing him somewhere private, even to that chilly barn—anywhere. *Damn the harbor eyes!*

Instead, I took the toy boat and went inside. A few seconds later, I opened the door, smiled at Todd, and waved.

Todd turned and walked the long way around to his home so Min and Eve would see he left me.

I took eight jugs of whiskey from the musty, granite-walled basement and hid them in the chicken coop. I then ate a cold bread and cheese supper, and quietly slid into bed next to a snoring Thaddeus.

Nobody would know what I had almost done. Yet part of me wanted to tell the world, I did! Being with Todd Calderwood like that was the most beautiful thing I had ever known.

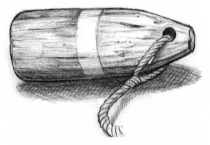

65

"Where'd this little gem come from?" Thaddeus asked the following morning. He held the carved peapod up and into the sun's rays pouring through the bay window. Watching from my perch on the bed, it looked like the vessel bounced along the harbor, the ocean's lumbering dark waves providing the perfect backdrop.

I looked at the peaceful scene with horror, recalling how Thaddeus's drunken drama at the schoolhouse had turned into my immoral escape at Todd's.

"Mighty fine boat, she is."

"Mr. Calderwood made it. He carved something for every child. This one is for our future little boy or girl. Or, for you."

"Even made my buoy, the right colors and everything. Oars row nice. Maybe that fella ain't so bad after all."

"Merry Christmas," I said, pained by his first kind words for Todd.

"Is Christmas?"

"That it is."

"Let's have at it, then! Got to make that new baby."

As he huffed and puffed, I squeezed my eyes shut, wishing to be with Todd.

"Oh no!" I yelled.

Thaddeus stopped. "What is it?"

"I just remembered I meant to bake some bread."

"You are a funny girl," quipped Thaddeus, and continued.

Oh no, I thought again, more to myself, for I wanted Todd to be the father.

"Oh Mildred," my husband finally groaned, rolling onto his back, "Mighty fine. Mighty fine."

We ventured downstairs when the sun was nearly at its height, Thaddeus holding onto his little toy boat.

While fried eggs and bacon sizzled and I made coffee, he continued to admire the model vessel sitting at the table. He held it up, *whooshing* it through imaginary waves. He picked up the buoy by its string and dropped it off the side of the boat. Then he set the boat down and rowed the oars with two hands, shaking his head and clicking his tongue in pleasant satisfaction.

"You really like that little carving."

"The first toy I ever had."

Startled, I dropped the plate of buns. The china broke, buns rolling off the table with half the plate, which broke again when it hit the floor.

"Be careful, Mildred!"

"Your first toy? You are nearly thirty-six years old!"

"Papa always said toys were for sissies."

"There is nothing wrong with a child playing! Children need to play."

"Not what my papa thought."

I wanted to cry as I picked up the pieces. My poor Thaddeus! "Never mind your father. You have your toy now. Better late than never."

"Maybe a boy of ours can have a few toys. Not too many, mind you. Ain't fathering no sissy."

"I could not imagine you doing so, dear," I said sadly, thinking how nice it would be to have a sensitive lad, a little boy I would cuddle when he so much as scraped his knee.

66

"Thaddeus, look outside!"

I relished the surprise distraction.

My entire world stood in front of our house, the harbor stretching behind them, a deep blue against the surrounding winter white: Lucy, Flo and Miles; Pearl, Orris, and Jon; Irville, Eve, Irv Junior, and Sam; Min and Marv; Rufus; and my Todd, his eyes anxiously sparkling.

All held bundles of food. I set our eggs and buns aside.

"Let them in, Thaddeus!"

Rosy-cheeked, smiling Hale Harbor folk entered, snow dripping onto the floor from boots and jackets. Flo had her fiddle, Irville his mandolin, and Marvin his accordion. Thaddeus pulled out his ukulele and started playing a welcome tune.

With each hug from the women and every nod from the fellas, even Todd's, I pushed my wicked actions of the previous afternoon from my mind.

Min and Todd helped me set up table extensions for our banquet in the dining room. I draped the table with the green-and-red tablecloth Ma had made special for my first Christmas away.

Quartet music filled the house. I imagined schooners and sloops creeping into the harbor in thick of fog, such happy melodies guiding their captains to safety.

"My muffins." Min proudly set her basket down.

"Don't they smell delicious."

"Wait until you taste the chocolate walnut brownies I made for dessert."

Eve followed with spaghetti and meatballs. Miles set a whole side of lamb on the table! Pearl added a lobster and green bean dish with a bowl of rice.

Rufus laid out three grilled mackerel on a flat piece of driftwood, and Todd displayed a toothy grin as he placed his hot dish on a folded towel. "Mushroom sauce. Might be good on Pearl's rice, or as a side dish."

"We are so blessed! Thank you all for coming."

"This is the most bestest Christmas ever!" Orris held Lucy's hands as the two danced in circles.

Added Eve, "And with some luck, next Christmas we'll have the littlest harbor child running around."

I looked at Todd, who just as quickly turned and picked up a muffin. I veered to Thaddeus, who grinned and then boasted, "A baby by next Christmas? We'll make one, a promise to you all. Maybe just did."

I dashed into the kitchen to fetch a knife for the lamb, feeling like a dagger had pierced my heart.

"No babe born nine months from now will be old enough to run about by Christmas!" I heard Min say with gusto, and most everybody laughed.

"Well, dig in." Thaddeus put down his ukulele. "Eat while it's hot."

The music stopped. Food evaporated fast. Todd sat far away from me.

Eve leaned back in her chair and patted her stomach. "You youngsters should make a snowman. We old folks have got to rest a bit while you run off what you've ate."

The children jumped to their feet. Orris's plate landed upside down on the floor. After grabbing coats and scarves and boots and hats, they skedaddled outside to a clear, sunny afternoon and lots of wet snow.

Todd and the gals cleared the table while the rest of the men huddled around the fire.

"Cards?"

"Sure, Thaddeus," Marv agreed. "But it's too early for rum."

"Yes, too early," agreed Thaddeus.

I looked at Todd again, who nodded with similar relief. His eyes had lost their sparkle. I wanted to hold his hand and assure him he was the sweetest experience of my life.

The boys settled into their game. Eve, Min, Pearl, Flo, Todd, and I dove into the kitchen work.

"Don't want to play cards, Todd?" asked Eve.

"Never been much for cards," he mumbled.

"Us neither," said Eve, not taking her eyes off him. "We are glad for your help. Mildred here should just sit, isn't that right? Too much work makes it harder to make that baby."

Todd turned beet-red.

"Gee Todd, am I embarrassing you? You must know about the birds and—"

"Bees. Yes, I know! Stop pressuring Mildred about babies!"

Todd's outburst silenced the girls. They had never seen him that way. Nor had I.

"Todd is right," Flora said after an awkward pause. "For heaven's sake, leave her be. She has one, she has one. She doesn't, she doesn't. We love Mildred May, with or without, just as we love Min."

Eve frowned at Flora, said nothing, then turned her back on us to dry dishes as noisily as anyone could.

Todd looked my way, eyes full of questions...or maybe just the one.

67

"What do you make of that?" I was in the barn bringing food scraps for the inside winter compost when I heard Thaddeus's voice, loud and clear. In the two-seater.

"Don't know." It was Jon!

I imagined, with the most intense disgust, two men pooping side by side while chatting.

"Jon, my Mildred's too smart for her britches, and as pushy as a yapping dog. Had no choice. Told her everything. Meant to tell you before, but Irv and Marvin always around."

"Will she keep our secret?"

"She will."

"The guilt is eating me up, Mr. Gale! Orris should know what I done to our father!"

"Don't cross me, Jon. Been protecting you, and Pearl, even Orris all this time, letting people think I offed Leroy. Hell, am glad people think I killed him! You say something now, though, you're done for. Me too, as—what do they call it?—accessory to you murdering? Pearl, too, she helped you with the body. Pearl and you in jail, now is that good for Orris?"

"Won't say nothing, I swear!"

Jon was crying. I hated Thaddeus most for that.

"Damn well better not."

"You wouldn't do anything to Mrs. Gale, would you, if she does tell someone?" Jon's voice quivered.

I stood still as a plank, barely breathing. It took Thaddeus a terrifyingly long time to answer.

"Jon, here's the damn truth of it. Couldn't never hurt my Mildred May, even if she slipped up about this. Am right fond of that woman. Now don't go telling anyone I said that."

"Won't say a word."

"Couldn't kill a woman anyways, no way, no how. But if she don't produce no babies—"

"You'd kill her for no babies?"

"No, you horse's ass! What do you think I am, some kind of monster?"

"What did you mean then, 'if she don't produce no babies'?"

"No babies, off island she goes."

"She will have some, am sure of it!" cried Jon.

I might not! I nearly screamed.

"Can't be sure. Need babies, goddamn it, this is serious! You're old enough. Pearl is not a blood relation."

"Pearl's been my mother almost as long as I can remember! I call her Ma!"

"You best start shopping around then, take trips up to Popplestone come spring, or Preacher Cove. Don't bother with Gooseneck."

"Am only sixteen."

"Almost seventeen. Old enough. You must know that by now."

"What about Mr. Calderwood, or Mr. Mank?"

"Useless blokes. Up to you and me."

"Will do my best, sir."

"We have two years to have another baby here. Mildred May or your girl our only chances. Mildred don't produce, she's out, and I'll have to try again with another wife."

"No!" Jon yelped what I wanted to shriek.

"Let's hope it don't come to that. I like her enough, that's for dang sure. Some days, I love her something fierce—never told nobody that but you, Jon."

"I won't tell. Am right glad you love her, Mr. Gale."

68

Earliest I could see Todd was two days later.

Thaddeus, again possessed by fear of running out of wood, took Irville, Marvin, and Jon back up Osprey Hill.

I ran.

Todd greeted me with surprise, and a cursory glance about the harbor.

I told him what I had heard in the barn, leaving out Thaddeus telling Jon how much he loved me.

"That man tries to kick you off the island, come straight here and live with me!"

"What would people say?"

"A lot of horrible things about us, you more, since you are the woman."

"Why, that's not fair."

"Never is, is how people are. It would not be easy, but we would manage."

"Unless we are both run off."

"There's that. I might have to buy a gun."

"Todd, no!"

"I am just so angry! He is treating you like chattel!"

"The harbor is hurting."

"Now you put the harbor before yourself, just like he does!"

"I am just being practical. How can I teach if there are no students after Lucy? Maybe he is right."

"He is not right. Thaddeus made a marital commitment to you, for life, no matter what comes—or doesn't come—your way."

"Thank you, Todd."

"Anyway, a lot can happen in six years, Mildred. Families could turn up. And Thaddeus is right about Jon being almost of age."

"Sixteen is awfully young."

"Seventeen isn't, and that's right around the corner for him."

"Or maybe Eve will have more."

"Exactly. Populating Hale Harbor is not your responsibility, Mildred."

"Seems as though it is, some days. And then there's still the killing of Leroy. That cannot be a secret forever."

"Maybe it can be. Maybe should be. Seems it has to be."

"So then Thaddeus gets credit for Leroy being gone, forever. He even encourages rumors that he killed him!"

"Ahh, my dear Mildred, of course he does."

"I do not understand."

"Because you are a woman."

"I am surprised you would say such a thing!"

"You misunderstand. Because you are a woman, you would never be so ridiculous, and I daresay narcissistic, as Thaddeus. He *wants* people to think he killed Leroy. Raises his already elevated status. Thaddeus is such a skunk!"

"My husband is not a skunk!"

Todd's face fell ashen then, and he lowered his head, "I am sorry, Mildred...maybe you should go."

"I am not leaving."

"Why are you here?"

"I need you."

"You have Thaddeus."

"I need you both."

"That is selfish. And inherently wrong."

"You were wrong, too!"

"Didn't seem wrong at the time. We talked about it. You convinced me."

"You didn't seem to need much convincing, Todd."

"Mildred May, you are being unfair! Can't you think of me now, of how I feel? And you are the married one, I am not! Oh God, I am sorry, I did not mean that, I swear!"

"You are right. I am the married one, so I am more at fault."

"I was just as wrong."

Neither of us said anything for a while. What used to be comfortable silence between us soaked with something awkward.

Todd finally said something. "We stopped, remember. It could have been worse."

"Worse would have been better for me."

"You honor me, Mildred."

"All this guilt and suffering, and we did not even really do it."

"We were right not to finish, we can feel good about that."

"I do not feel good about that."

"I see that now. And I am sorry for how you are feeling. How about we talk about Jon for a bit?"

"All right."

"Thaddeus said he was protecting Jon from arrest, right? Well, having Jon in his pocket is worth a lot to your Thaddeus. This harbor is basically his."

"I wish *you* were mine, not Thaddeus."

Todd cross his arms. "You have a very odd...downright mean way of showing that, Mildred."

"Todd, I did not want to so soon after we—"

"But you did."

"That was not my choice."

"Oh my God, no. He—"

"No, not like that, but I let him, I...I did not say no, felt I had to, would have been difficult to explain why I would not be agreeable... in that moment...but I promise you I did not start it up! I did not want to! I was resigned to it. That is the honest truth, Todd."

"This is all my fault, Mildred. I've made things tough for you at home now."

"Things were already tough for me at home."

"How can I help?"

"There is something."

"I will do anything."

"Is much more than a bookshelf."

"Figured. Ask me."

"Keep trying with me to increase the odds I get pregnant."

"Mildred May!"

"I mean it! Todd, that husband of mine said I have two years to produce a whole baby! What will happen if I do not get pregnant within a year? I love this harbor and everyone in it. I want a baby, too. I want *your* baby most! Can we not, for the good of the harbor and for us, and because we want to, keep on trying? Thaddeus made four families leave because of the barren ones. You must help me!"

"You would sleep with two men at the same time for the good of the harbor?"

"Yes...yes, I guess I would. And mostly because I love you."

"Not right at all."

"But we almost did it once! Again is the same, nothing worse. Already there, so, I mean, why not again then? Why are you making me beg?"

A long silence followed my plea.

"Oh no, Todd, I am scaring you away when I want you to swoop me up and kiss me again."

"You are not scaring me. I am scaring myself." He took a deep breath. "Mildred, there is something I must tell you. This is something I have never told anyone."

"I can keep your secret."

"This is an enormous secret. Maybe bigger than Jon's."

"You have killed someone?"

"No! Nothing bad. Well, I do not think it is bad. It isn't."

"I will keep your secret, Todd."

Todd held my hands tighter. His face appeared older, strained.

"Todd?"

"Mildred, this is hard to tell you."

"I am listening. You can tell me anything, you know that."

"You deserve to know...my trips to Portland are...to see a very special someone."

The floor seemed to fall out from under my feet. I tried to pull away. He held on. Grasping my hands like that was the most aggressive thing I ever experienced from Todd.

"Why did you sleep with me, then? Oh God, I must go!"

"No! Hear me out, Mildred! I loved you that afternoon. I love you now."

"But you cannot, you know, continue? You have someone! How could you do that to me? How could you do that to *her*?"

"Mildred, how dare you judge me?"

"I know, but—!"

"But what?"

"I hate the thought of it!"

"What do you want? Both me and Thaddeus, happily ever after?"

Neither of us said anything for a while.

"Yes, I want happily ever after with both of you. I deserve that, I do."

"You cannot. That would never really work."

"I do not see why not."

"You are so stubborn."

"Why does everyone say that?"

"Because it is true."

"What is wrong with the three of us happy, somehow?"

"Besides the obvious, there is more, and maybe, just maybe, this will help you, and me."

"I do not like where this is going, but I'm listening."

Todd took another deep breath. Caressed my hand.

"My special someone is a man. Close friend. Best friend...lover. We have been together for a long time. We are...that is, we consider ourselves...married. I betrayed him when I was with you. I have never dishonored nor disrespected him before. I do not regret yours and my time together, is just that..."

As he paused, I pictured Todd naked with a man as beautiful as he, only different. That image made me want him even more, and my face flushed.

"I embarrass you. I am so sorry, Mildred."

"It is not embarrassment. And I am very glad you are not with another woman. That somehow makes this easier for me."

"You do not think I am...um...strange?"

"You are not strange. You are different."

"I love him, Mildred! We are going on ten years now. When I said I was as much at fault as you were being married, I meant it."

"But, what you and I did!"

"I will always treasure what we did. And you and I want a baby, something he and I cannot do. This was all, well, it sounds ridiculous, stupid, and crazy right now, but is all what I thought. My friend may forgive me for the one time and because, you know, we did not quite... do everything. But if you and I, um, continue, I will never have hope for the lifelong happiness I believe I have found with him."

Todd put his head in his hands, spoke softly. "He is all the family I have left. I cannot lose him, Mildred."

In that moment, I envied Todd something fierce. Todd's friend seemed to really be his, as I had wanted Thaddeus, or Todd, or both, to really be mine. I had neither, it seemed, not completely.

Todd put more wood in the potbelly, causing it to roar, as I responded, "I am disappointed...I mean, I am happy for you...and him, but I wish...oh the thought of not being with you like that again... Todd, Christmas Eve was the sweetest afternoon of a lifetime! To think never again! I just cannot bear it."

"I am sorry. Flattered, too. Truly honored."

I sighed. "Life is so complicated."

"It is. Mildred, I have held this close to my heart my whole life. I feel a gigantic weight lifting just by telling you. I wish I could tell everyone! But, my dear, is knowing this too much of a burden on you?"

"Not a burden. I am trying to adjust. I still do not understand, I mean, you could, with me. You...your drawers!"

"I have never had such an experience with a woman. Actually, I have only had two boyfriends my whole life. My friend and I are— were—very loyal."

"I was your first?"

"Well actually, yes, my first woman. Or rather, my almost woman."

"Well maybe you just do not know how it is, long term! Maybe a man got to you first. How do you know?"

"I know. Have known since I was fourteen."

"Oh."

"Didn't *do* anything, mind you! At first, just thoughts. And then it became obvious when things happened to me when I looked at boys I liked. Never had those feelings with girls, or women."

"Until me."

"Until you."

"I like that. Makes me feel special."

"You *are* special. Being with you, Mildred May, was something unusual. I could have you know, I am sure of it."

"I wish we had, seems that was my one and only chance."

Todd smiled then, the most blushing smile I have ever been complimented with.

"That you are beautiful and unusual was clear the moment you rowed into Hale Harbor wearing a wedding dress and fishing boots."

"I must have been quite a sight."

"Indeed you were, and are."

"Todd, I need to tell you that, while I will keep your secret, it may not be much of one."

"Oh?"

"People talk. The girls, well, way back in September, that night Thaddeus threw Leroy off the porch, they told me they thought you were sweet on guys. I did not believe it at the time and told them so."

"I see."

"I am sorry."

"Don't be. It is for the best. What about Hale Harbor men?"

"Well, they are not as kind, but no real harm, either. Just being silly about things, as far as I can tell."

"I haven't been run off. Some places, I would be."

"Sounds like you know that from experience."

"We should have known not to move to a town named Purgatory. The fear of being run off again is why my friend has not moved out here with me."

"Your fella should move here! He would make Hale Harbor seventeen!"

"Eighteen if you have a baby."

"Even better. A solid dozen and a half."

"Pains us both we've had to live apart. But since the move brought me here to a stunning harbor's edge, and to you, I am content. He has a good job in Portland. Someday maybe he can be here. I would like that very much."

"We would all like that very much, including me—especially me."

"Thank you, Mildred."

"Todd, I am grateful you shared this deep secret of yours. About your friend. I am...touched, honored. I hope to someday meet your... your beau. Please, what is his name?"

Todd lit up like a five-year-old seeing his birthday cake.

"Stuart Charles Pendleton is his name! You are the first to ask or know! Stuart has never met my parents, brothers, or sister. My sister walked in on my first boyfriend and me together at my parents' house years ago. I have not been welcome home since. I do not even dare go back by myself."

"No!"

"My father took it especially hard. He said he never wanted to see me again. My brothers, well, they were disgusted. One called me revolting. My sister just seemed distraught, wishing she hadn't seen us, or had said anything. It was horrible. My mother cried. I caused them all so much pain!"

Todd's voiced cracked and he wiped a tear, adding, "I tell you, my father meant what he said about never wanting to see me again. My nieces and nephews were little then, so I've not been part of their lives either. Some of them probably do not even know I exist. So you see, Stuart has not met anyone else important to me. That is one of the great losses for men like us, that those who are most special in our hearts are rarely part of, or even known by, family."

"You have not met his family, either?"

"No, we fear the same result."

"That is terrible. Not right. Their loss, too. And it is settled then!

Your Mr. Stuart C. Pendleton and I must meet. Soon. We will make it so."

"As long as he forgives me."

"Must you tell him? I mean, it was not real."

"Mildred, you know darn well it was real, even as we did not consummate. I owe him the truth."

"From what you have told me about Stuart, he will forgive you. I hope he forgives me, too. You can both be doting uncles to my daughter or son."

"Dearest Mildred, do you really think so?"

I daresay I saw a few tears from him, joyful tears of hope.

Those tears brightened the light blue of Todd's eyes. I loved the man so much then, I could let him go.

"Yes, Todd, I really think so."

Out on his front steps, with a twinkle in his eye and a quick glance into the fields and harbor, Todd leaned over and softly kissed my cheek. I grasped his shirt lapels with two hands, pulling him close. I kissed him on the lips, closing my eyes so I could smell him that deeply for the last time.

Then we hugged, staying in that embrace for what I wished could be forever.

"Mildred!"

Thaddeus stomped inside, shards of ice-packed snow slipping off his trousers and jacket, shattering as they hit the floor. Every corner of the house whistled with the arrival of our first major winter storm. Skies darkened. Windows rattled.

I pulled a jar of pickled vegetables from the cabinet in the kitchen. "Yes, Thaddeus?"

The man took hold of me and twisted me around to face him. The jar slipped out of my fingers and smashed into pieces on the floor, juice splashing my ankles.

He was about to push me, yet again.

I looked Thaddeus hard in the eye and searched for the man far better than his God-awful shoving. He was there, somewhere, had to be, because I was stuck with him.

"Remember what your father told you about how to treat a woman!"

"My father did not catch my mother with another man!"

"What are you talking about?"

"You know what I'm talking about. Wouldn't be the first time a harbor girl strayed. That Eve, well sure as sugar, Sam's not Irv's, just look at the boy!"

"Looks mean nothing."

"She's been with that Smith fella, saw them smooching just as sure as I saw you and Calderwood cuddling up outside his house!"

"You are spying on me?"

"Seen you two clear as day from Osprey Hill. Killed a man once. I can kill a man again."

"Only in yours and everyone else's fool head did you kill a man."

"Could've! And would have, if Jon hadn't beat me to it."

"I am keeping your arrogant—that means cocky—murdering secret. On one condition. No, two conditions."

"Christ, Mildred! What are they?"

"One, you support me in Todd being my friend. A friend is all. Nothing more."

"I do not like him!"

"Then learn to."

"What if I cannot?"

"You can if you try. Think about the thoughtful carving he made. Even as a gift to our child, that little boat he so carefully made was all about honoring you and your livelihood."

"You've a point there, maybe Todd ain't all bad."

"Nobody is all bad."

"But he touched you! Kissed you! You kissed him back! On the lips!"

"Kissing him on the lips will not happen again. Nor anything beyond that."

"A promise?"

"A promise."

"I will not be made a fool of."

"I know. And I understand your feelings, Thaddeus, I really do."

"So, let me get this straight. You want everything with Todd except...except...damn it, Mildred, don't make me say it!"

"Exactly, everything but sex. A friend, is all. What is so hard for you about me having a male friend?"

"Have you—"

"We have never, I assure you."

"Then he really is a—"

"Not saying. You just have to trust us."

Thaddeus frowned and then nodded, slowly.

"And the second condition: No matter how long it takes you and me to have a baby, or even if we manage no babies at all, I am staying here, with you, in Hale Harbor."

"Mildred May, this here harbor needs babies, or we won't survive!"

"I will do my best. But how can I promise such a thing? Is up to God."

"Is a hell of a lot more up to you and me than God! You will... with me...won't you?"

"Yes. When and how often I like."

Thaddeus groaned. "And how often will that be?"

"Well that, dear husband, depends on how kind and fair you are to me, and how kind and fair you are to others. Then there is how tired I am from chores, things like that. The point is, I am not at your beck and call. I will when I want to, assuming you want to. We are good together sometimes. Let's be like that—good—always, if you please."

"But I always want to."

"I know, but Thaddeus, I do not always want to. I definitely do not want to *have to*. I want to, though, in a regular enough way—you must know this about me by now."

"I see. You hold all the cards, then, for the bedroom."

"That I do, and that I must. All women need to be like that."

"Next thing, you'll be demanding to vote."

"Maybe so. I deserve a voice at home. I deserve a voice in America, too."

Thaddeus smiled, the kind of grin he had before he turned so crusty and sometimes mean.

"Knew you was strong, Mildred! And I'd like my vote to count twice, with you voting, too."

"I might vote the same as you, and then again, I might not."

My husband laughed. "You sure are independent."

"I am an island girl, never been off an island, not once, 'course I am independent."

"You didn't want to get in the boat after our wedding, did you, island girl?"

"I did not."

"But you did."

"Yes."

"Are you glad, even with everything you know now, that you got into my boat?"

"Yes, I am glad."

"Well then, woman, I believe we have a deal, your heavy conditions and all."

"And for the last time telling you, call me Mildred or Mildred May, or even Mrs. Gale, if you like, never 'woman,' and especially not 'my woman'!"

"Okay, got it, I will remember, Mrs. Mildred May Combs Gale."

"A promise?"

"A solid promise."

"Well now, that is all good!" I brushed my hand along his dark hair and behind his big ear. "I would not want to have to go after you with an iron skillet."

"Me neither. I see now I would not come out well on the other end of that, just like Big Leroy. Was right, always am! You are one strong woman Mildred May, is why the hell I wanted to marry you. Yes sir, was right all along...always was, always am, always will be."

"Thaddeus Francis Gale!"

"You adding another condition?"

"No, Mr. Gale, I am not."

"Then what?"

"I know something about you. You must remember it, always."

"What?"

"You are better than your father. And that means you will be a better husband, and a better father, than he was."

"Do you really believe that?"

I daresay I saw a few tears from him, happy tears of hope. Those tears brightened the deep blue of Thaddeus's eyes. I loved the man enough then, I thought I could keep him.

"Yes, Thaddeus, I do."

———❧

Josiah Charles Gale came into the world near midnight of September 23, 1913, screaming as fiercely as the southerly storm slamming sea spray against the turret windows of his birthing room.

With my baby boy and Stuart C. Pendleton making us eighteen, a new chapter began in Hale Harbor. I am so very tired now from those many years, resting my pen on the desk in what was my son and daughters' first room starting sixty years ago.

My oh my, so much happened living on the end of Popplestone Isle. I want to tell the world, I do!

I will share those stories next, if they are ones you would like to hear, and if I live long enough. Or perhaps I will convince my dear son-in-law Orris to tell them instead.

—Mildred May Combs Gale, age 88, December 26, 1973

Kate Hotchkiss

In addition to authoring the On Harbor's Edge series, Kate is a freelance writer, classic model, and photographer with contributions to online and print magazines, newspapers, books, and commercial advertisements. Her writings and photographs mostly relate to Maine island sustainability and appear in *Maine Boats, Homes & Harbors, National Fisherman, Island Journal, Weekly Waterfront, Isle au Haut Engine, Maine Island Living*, and more.

Kate raised two boys and is empty nesting with husband Ellard and their sons' pets. Prior to creative writing, she enjoyed decades of business with Asia via the private sector, government service, and the United Nations. Kate has lived on Hong Kong and Maine islands since 1998, with the exception of two years in Beijing.

As a Vermont youngster, Kate discovered magic in Maine by finding a dark pouch that protects a shark or skate embryo—a mermaid's purse.